COAST PLAYA'S

by

Antonio Berry

COAST PLAYA'S

Published by

Midnight Express Books
POBox 69
Berryville AR 72616
http://MidnightExpressBooks.com
(870) 210-3772

Email: MEBooks1@yahoo.com

Coast Playa's

Copyright © 2012 Antonio Berry
ISBN-10: 0988806304
ISBN-13: 978-0-9888063-0-6

Disclaimer: This is a work of fiction. All characters are totally from the imagination of the author and depict no persons, living or dead; any similarity is totally coincidental.

To get in touch with the author, you may write him at:
Antonio Berry
P.O. Box 8025
Moss Point, MS 39562-8025

Published by
Midnight Express Books
POBox 69
Berryville AR 72616
http://MidnightExpressBooks.com
(870) 210-3772
Email: MEBooks1@yahoo.com

COAST PLAYA'S

ACKNOWLEDGMENTS

This book is written not to give up the game or the way the game was played by the coldest playa's that ever played it, but to clear the myth for my family, children, grandchildren and even those that have no idea that Tony Berry was not just an alleged drug dealer. Most people have only heard rumors and remember the drug tales but never came into the truth that contributed to the intricate role in the grooming of the man that became known across the country in many states and cites as Bro-n-Law, or Freddy. The true story needed to be told in order to form a more factual and complete conclusion of the individual that's being talked so much about. It is so often that half the story is told with many twist and missing details until in the end nobody knows the complete truth.

My family never had the opportunity to hear directly from me concerning my traveling on the road in and out of different states doing what I was doing at the time. Hopefully this will shed some light for them. It's graphic and has explicit language but it was necessary for the truthfulness of the state of mind at that particular time in my life.

To my Mother Shirley, Father Johnnie, Aunt Vera and Uncle Billy. My Brothers, Eric and Darryl, and Sister Sharon. My Children Andraya, Tony, Antrice and Tara. Grand-children, Christian, Swa'drian, Jashun, Centrell, Nylan,Jordan, Keelan, And AJ aka L'il Tony III. Love you all.

I'd also like to thank the following people and let them know that my thoughts and prayers go out to them:

Anthony (Goodie) Morrison	Bettie Wells	Kevin Myles
Michael Berry (Nephew)	Edward Grimes	Calvin Lindsey
Antonio Johnson	Tisha Johnson	Ossie McCauley
Charles(Red)Johnson	Arlean Johnson	Eric Peagler

Delrick Pettway	Celidore Nelson	Edmond Brown
William (GA) Howard	Eloise Nelson	Eric Adams
Timmy Ware	Jacquelin Nelson	Lazurus Reeves
Nathan Carter	Marka McCoy	Jerome Harris
Marvin Griffin	Zelda Andrews	Jerry Knight
JK "Mr. Move the Work"	Alfred Collins	
Thedford Sylvester	David Daniels	Thresea Snowden
Reginald Williams	Andres Miranda	
"Chop Po" Ervin Holloway		Kendrick Terrell
David Zebroski	Chanda B.Taylor	
Reginald Williams	Hub-City "Smooth"	Wanda Rankins
Brian Pearson	Ke-Ke Paul "R.I.P."	Lawrence James
Timothy Dandridge	Lacurtus Dunn	Rita Lampton
Brian Pearson	Chatt"Mello"	Marie Carter
Kevin Jones	Houma"Deon"	Landy Thomas
Nathaniel Bailey	Jose Vazquez	Sharon Thomas
Michael Gordon	Angelle Vonderpool	Julian Smith
Tyrone Richardson		
Selma "Cougar Head"	Troyell "Turk" Ross	John Lee
Aaron Pendergrass	Erik Bozeman	Edward King
Andre Mays	Cuong Pham	
Donald Jackson	Steve Paul	Bruce Simmons
Willie Reed	Willie Mathis	Tory Chester

Chapter 1

Tac! Tac! Tac! Bullets are flying and ricocheting everywhere while the breaking of glass causes teeth to grit and souls to pray all in the mist of bodies falling and running recklessly in no certain direction hoping not to become a victim of what society has cultivated and forced into one of many poverty zones of the great divided state of America. An older model blue Delta Oldsmobile pulls off leaving the smell of rubber fuming the air and hearts beating like drums. Sirens echo in the distance as pedestrians and residents alike lift their heads and bodies in an attempt to understand the mayhem that has transpired and often raises its ugly head in Carver Village on Live Oak Ave in the city of Pascagoula, Mississippi, home of the Coast Playa's.

There are several disable automobiles parked curb-side that on any given cold night allow the homeless a decent night's sleep. Some are a total loss as a result of the gangsta show that had transpired only seconds ago. What is even more obvious are the two shadows, barely recognizable, slumped over in the primer-gray '65 Ford Galaxy 500.

The driver's door opened with a sudden horror scream, "Help me please, somebody help us!" The driver, Aaron, is hit and said this in a voice so faint that an audiometer is needed to hear it over the drowning of his own blood. The passenger Troy is also badly wounded and is not moving.

The ambulance pulled up and immediately began to perform life saving techniques on Troy in an effort to deny him a formal introduction to his maker. An old lady walked by and looked down on the pavement at the sprawled bleeding figure and said, "Lord he's only a child. These kids are killing one another as a form of recreation."

The ambulance drove off in the direction of Singing River Hospital and the activities of the day continue. These events will not stop what must take place to survive in what's better known as "the trenches".

Its 7:30 a.m. on a cloudy Saturday in late April of 1991. The wind is still and as a usually morning habit, I decided to cruise through the 'hood of Carver Village in my Candy Green 300 E. AMG Benz observing the destruction of the night before caused by the dope fiends, pimps, hustlers, and gangsta's who own this element of life. The despair that I witness is one that society is intentionally doing but would like to ignore and pretend it's the predators fault and is the reason for such poverty and hopelessness in their lives. I believe it is just a repeat of what happened in South Central, Los Angeles back in the early '90s.

Carver Village is a project home that sits across the street from a strip of clubs. It's also a Ho track where prostitutes walk 24/7 and in between any rain drops that may fall while tricking trying to catch their Johns. Their Pimp's main theme is, "Bitch better have my money straight."

Hustlers from all over the country come to Carver Village to hustle. To name a few: Corey, aka Ironhead, from River City, Miami, Panamanians Alex and Alvin and Keith, from new York, Florida Tony from Tampa, Lucky, Duncan and Philly Dog from the West Coast Cali Crew and the rest is a mixture and too many more to name. Whatever one desires in the world; from gun drama to sex or getting high, it can be found in the Village. Weed, cocaine, and dope are easy to find but the village offers very little hope for the victims of that bad Gorilla called a Jones.

The games played by the hustlers and playas off the Coast of Mississippi range from short change (Noting), drag, slumming, all the way up to hypnosis with the instruction for the mark to enter a bank and to return with the cheese. If one is to get caught sleeping on this coast you're subject to one of two options; broke or bagged, because the foundation and rules that has been laid has no discriminations. More killings have happened on this front than the war front of Vietnam not to mention the numerous times the Grim Reaper has visited directly inside the project home itself to claim its victims. No matter what geographical area of the Earth one comes from, Carver Village in Pascagoula, Mississippi leaves an everlasting belief that it's a war zone city inside a city with its own laws.

If a Hustler was able to get down in Carver Village and make it out alive to become older, they're groomed to go anywhere in the four corners of the world and survive. This was the environment of the village at one time. There's a three feet wall meant to separate and shield the residents from all the horror, mischief and screams of the clubs and street. Day and night life scenes take place only a few yards away from where citizens reside.

As I'm cruising down Live Oak Street, the street in which the Village sits, I hear someone scream, "Yo Freddy!"

Very few people call me Tony, its either Freddy or Bro-n-law. So I quickly turned in the direction of the voice and notice one of the youngest hustlers in the hood name Germaine. He's sitting on the three feet wall spiting and popping game at the mud kickers who are still walking the beat with all the signs of having been out all night trying to meet their pimp's quota.

Germaine is a slim young brother of about 20 years in age, 5'10", and 150lb with a mild complexion and dresses every day as if he's modeling for a fashion magazine. The brother is a true sport and comes from a blood line of hustlers and pimps. The brother keeps a stable of ethnicity females at his disposal. At the age of 15 Germaine was the youngest jit on the block pushing a Jaguar. For this reason, and for the way he carried himself, I've always felt comfortable having him around and doing whatever I could for him. He would try a thing or two but he gave respect to where it was due. The youngsta had some class.

"What's up Germaine?"

"Ain't nothing happening Freddy. Just chillin' watching and trying to trick one of these broads for their trap money and keep them beating their feet. Check this out, be careful how you roll through, because this strip is hotter than Tucker was when his daddy died and left him broke. It's no joke up through here right about now. Some shooting went on last night and L'il Troy was sprayed from chest down and his crime partner Aaron was hit in the shoulder, back and stomach. They still haven't arrested anybody for the shooting and they're looking in every alley. Troy is still in ICU fighting to see another B-Day. What do you have to puff on?" He asked.

"I got a couple of joints, hop in and let's bend one," I replied.

Chapter 2

I was raised in a home of three boys and one girl; Eric, Darryl, Sharon and myself with me being the oldest of the four. Like any other typical young black boy growing up in this era, I was bad and hard headed. Although I was surrounded and shown plenty of love from Mama, Big Mama, Grand-daddy, MuDear, Aunt Vera and Uncle Billy I still insisted on doing things my way. This was hard for them to understand because I was an A and B student in school. They had wished and hoped that I would attend college and become a successful man in corporate America or just prosperous period.

Every one of them spent quality time with me trying to keep me on the right path. Grand-daddy would take me to his places of businesses and had even given me jobs during the summer and took me on trips. Billy did everything from attempting to teach me, Eric, and Darryl Karate, to coaching us in football and would occasionally supervise us swimming in the pool at Grand-daddy and Mudear's house in the pool that was built especially for the family and family gatherings. Billy has always been the most admired and respected male member of our family. He could always be counted on for sound advice and what was more important fairness. He and Aunt Vera was the shining example in the family of what marriage is suppose to be.

My mom Shirley had to have incredible strength to raise three boys that was as bad as we were but she managed and did well. We never missed a meal or went without clothing and shoes. There never was a cold or hungry night. We always had plenty and looking back we was somewhat spoiled. She kept us in league football, basketball and baseball. She did this all while having to force my daddy to pay child support which he did very rarely if at all. So my hat goes off to her.

My Dad wasn't all that bad and I've always had a relationship with him even when I didn't fully understand the affairs of him and my mom. What I can say is that as we got older and I guess as daddy got older also he seen the error of his ways because he did try and make amends for not being there, so I give him his props also. It's this saying, "No matter where and when you're saved the point is you're there now and that's what counts."

*****

The day of graduation had finally crept upon me and mama had once again been there for me by purchasing a Toyota Celica Gt for me with the anticipation and hope that I would be attending college when August arrived. By this time my High School sweet heart Venus was pregnant and, unbeknownst to Mama, I had no intentions to attend any college when the summer was over. All I could think about is the sense of freedom and all that came with it. With Venus being pregnant and having to see a doctor regularly, I resorted to the trade of selling marijuana to help pay the doctor bills for our unborn child. With the money also came other women, so I'm having too much fun when August arrived to even think about anything else; especially not college. If I were to agree to go to college I would once again become dependent on my parents and family and subjected to their rules and beliefs. At this time I'm also suspicious that I could be the father of another child. Whenever I would see the mother of this child I'd always inquire with her whether or not I'm the father. Her answer would always be the same. No you're not her father; her father's name is Hollis. I would always let it go at that because I have not yet seen the little girl.

It was hard telling Mama that I had changed my mind and wasn't going to college, so I let her figure it out on her own as it came time for me to be getting my gear together to leave in the next couple of weeks. When Mama figured out I wasn't going anywhere all hell broke lose and she made it clear that I was going to do something with my life or get from underneath her roof. Since I thought I had reached the age and maturity to make such an important decision on my own without consulting with her and my Stepfather Richard, after all the time and effort had been placed in the preparation of me leaving for college, well, I could just find someplace to live. I had no other choice and had to come up with a plan and real soon too because mama was putting the full court press down like a mafia don.

My Stepfather Richard met my Mom when I was around six years old and did for us as if we were his own. He fed and clothed us and provided all that a father should. He also spoiled us rotten and sometimes would keep Mama off us. He was always willing to help further all of our education.

The idea I come up with was to enlist in the military, the United states Army. I enlisted October 22, 1982; almost a month after Li'l Tony was born. I did not remain in the military for any length of time worthy of detailing. I did basic training in Fort Knox, Kentucky and AIT (63 Whisky) in Aberdeen, Maryland. I enlisted on the 'Buddy Plan' with a friend name Aaron who at the time enlisted in the marines. In December 1982 after the completion of basic training we were given a Xmas holiday break for leave to visit home before reporting to our next duty station. Venus, Turk and my cousin Paula arrived at Fort Knox to take me home for the holidays. Turk pulled up on the base in his green Cadillac Seville. The desire to sex Venus was too strong for me to wait the couple more hours it would take for us to reach home. I insisted we stop in Birmingham, AL to stay overnight. The pay I was earning a month was less than what I sometimes made in a week on the streets. My arrival date to Aberdeen was the first week in January 1983. To cure the problem with the pay and make it easier to support Venus and Li'l Tony, Venus and I decided to get married before I returned to duty. This immediately doubled my pay to $1,100 a month.

AIT duty was going well for me and all the Drill Sergeants were pleased with my performance. The problem didn't occur until I discovered that my next duty would be in Korea where you weren't allowed to bring your family. This did not set well with me and I immediately begin to devise a plan of execution out of the service. After brief periods of interviews with some top brass and on one occasion informed them that I would not fight under any circumstances and would remain in my fox hole during a time of war, I was finally released with a General Discharge under Honorable Conditions.

I'm home now doing nothing with Mama constantly on me about the decisions I've made. I decided to call Venus so we could decide on what to do next because it's too late to cry about it now and time to move on and do what has to be done.

"Hello, yeah this me, get up I'm on my way to pick you up."

 Venus, who was living with her mom in Pascagoula, said, "Tony do you know what time it is?"

"Yes, I know what time it is and need for you to get up because I have something that's important that I need to discuss with you. I'll be there in about thirty minutes," I said.

"Tony what is going on that you had to wake me up at 4:30 in the morning?" she asked.

"I've been out all night contemplating what to do about our situation and the options Mama and I argued about a few hours ago. Venus you know I don't want to and will not go to College and leave you and Lil Tony here to struggle while I'm off living on my parents not worried about any bills, diapers, milk or the raising of our child. Mama said I could get ready to go to school since I've came back from the army or get from under her roof and take care of myself. So, I've been thinking all night and I believe we can do this on our own and make it work. With you working and me on the grind, we'll be alright," I told her.

"Tony are you sure? Because you know your family will blame me." said Venus.

"We'll worry about that later. I'll be back around 10:00 so we can ride and look for us a spot."

Chapter 3

Lil' Tony was born September 27, 1982 and several months afterward on my return from the army we found ourselves a one bedroom apartment at Lakeside Manor.

Lakeside caters to half local residents and half naval personal.

At this point in time I'm selling weed and riding around every day trying to catch a trick to add to my already small bank roll. Turk had put me down with a few pieces of slum jewelry to sell that would eventually change the course of my life and take me places beyond anything I had anticipated and I was loving it.

Everybody was healthy and happy. I was thinking things could not be better. I'm 18 years old and my own man with a cash flow that allows me to do whatever I choose to do. If I decided to get out of bed in the morning, it's cool; if not, that's cool, too.

L'il Tony, aka Man, is my little fellow. There's not a moment during the day that I don't think about him and can't wait to get back to the house to play and cuddle with him. He cries when I leave the house without him. I love being with him so much that most days, I pick him up early from the baby-sitter and we're already home when Venus arrives from work.

It still wasn't clear whether or not I'm the father of the other child that the streets are screaming about. This is a constant thought that's taking up a place in my mind and heart.

Turk, Venus' sister Sabrina's boyfriend, is a flat-foot hustler originally from Pensacola, Florida and has lived in Mississippi for the past 5 or 6 years. The brother is having it his way; money, cars and the baddest popular broads in the town.

Turk is a dark-complexion brother, 5'10", 180 pounds with the gift of gab and makes you think that the slum game was tailor-made just for him. He's a good brother with a heart of gold; one of those people that has a way of saying things and making them sound funny when it's really not. This Brother rides around in his money-green, 79 Cadillac Seville catching tricks for five grand or better a day.

Turk introduced me to the slum game of selling knock-off rings, chains, bracelets and imitation designer watches even before I graduated from high school. The slum game increased my ability to make more money by placing another notch under my belt in the world of grinding.

People will tell you and speak as if they know all about this game of selling fake jewelry because they have been approached many times by guys trying to sell it to them. I bet you before you go any further reading my story, that what they know isn't remotely close to what I'm going to reveal to you concerning the way we were playing the game across the country.

When you think you know everything or all there is to know about a subject, in reality you know nothing at all.....which will be proven as you read on.

I'm now riding from place to place in town trying to catch a trick to help keep food on the table and rent paid for Venus, L'il Tony and myself while ducking throwing bricks at the state Penitentiary.

I have not yet perfected the skill of going in and out of businesses. After a long, hard day trying to catch a good trick and only having $200.00 for my all day effort, I call it a day and head for the house frustrated because the tricks weren't biting today. I'm a rookie in this game but if I get up and start my mission at 8:00 a.m., by 11:00-12:00 p.m., I'd expect to have caught a good trick and be riding, kicking the game and smoking some good weed.

As I walked through the door, Venus has beaten me home from work from her 9-to-5 job.

Before I could get a drink of water, she's telling me that Turk came by and said for me to pass through the village and holla at him.

I told Venus to call Sabrina and let Turk know that I'm on my way because I wasn't hanging in the village and I don't care too much about getting caught there.

All I could think about and hope for is that Turk hadn't come across one of my tricks because sometimes that could spell trouble.

As I'm rolling through the hood of the village, I notice Turk standing on the corner of the club named Hide Away Lounge with a beer in his hand talking to another guy. "Yo, whats up Turk?"

"Park and get out, I need to holla at you," said Turk. "You must have been working this area kind of strong," he said.

"Yeah, why?"

"Sabrina and I had a fight and she called the police. While I was lying in bed sleep, they woke me up by hitting me on the feet and telling me I'm arrested for domestic violence and needed to come with them. At first sight, it tripped me out because I was thinking it might have been the cause of a trick, but that is not what I needed to holla at you about. While I was signing the bail papers, one of the white officers leaned across the counter at the station getting real close to my face, so close that I could smell his tobacco breath. He said that I needed to talk to that little young, light-complexion Negro boy that's riding around in that red Toyota selling that junk to his people before somebody kills him. Before he could finish, I knew he was talking about you Tony and said to myself that one of his buddies must have bit and bit real good because he looked as if he wanted to come across the counter and take it out on me and probably would have under different circumstances. Turk you know me; I'm going to ask any and everybody that cross my path while I'm trying to eat. You know this game is not based on sympathy and it's not even a thought when it comes to asking one of these Caucasians."

"Listen Tony," said Turk. "If you want, you can hit the road with me this weekend when I pull out again. I'm going to Texas and think it would be better for you to work the road than around here where you live if you're trying to get some real money and plus we have almost burned this area up."

Now I'm really excited and said, "Hell yeah. When are you going to come to pick me up???"

Turk said that he'd come by this Saturday and we'd turn a few corners and leave Sunday night so we can be somewhere first thing Monday morning getting in some work........

Chapter 4

It's Sunday, June, 1983, 8:00pm and the sun hadn't been long set on a 95 degree summer day with the flow of traffic moving to the blast of car stereos. Tops and windows alike are in the down position. People are listening to the songs 777-9311 and The Gap Band Burn Rubber On Me, The Isley Brother's Choosey Lover and Luther Coming Out. Turk pulls up and hit the world wide famous pimp blow. The three quick peck of the horn back to back. I kissed Venus and L'il Tony on my way out the door and tell her I'll call as soon as we touchdown.

"Let's hit it so we can be somewhere trying to catch us a trick when the sun comes up in the morning," said Turk.

Turk is a professional con-man that hasn't punched a working man clock in more than 5 years and when he stumbled upon the slum game, there wasn't a slummer around that could match his game. Only one came close and that was a guy name Mickey. Turk was getting dope money in the slum game - I mean real dope money without throwing bricks at the penitentiary. Turk gave me, Snap, Rodney, Dwight and his brother Jeff the game and schooled us along the way until we was able to perfect the technique and swim in the ocean of fish on our own, he actually took me to work day-to-day with him.

We headed west on I-10 towards Louisiana with our destination being Beaumont, Texas. Beaumont is four and a half hours give or take a few minutes from Pascagoula, Mississippi. Beaumont is a water costal town same as Pascagoula/Moss Point with about an area population of 150,000; the neighboring city of Port Arthur being the next largest city. They call the geographic short Texas. After a good night of rest, I wake up and step just out-side the hotel door to the smell of an industrial city with refineries and other manufacturing plants.

I'm trying to grasp and imagine this new setting to me for a determination of what kind of economic potential this place could have on me and my families future as far as a bank roll is concerned because that's my main reason for being in this spot in the first place. So far the scenery looks and smells rich.

Traffic is moving at a fast pace as if everyone is in a hurry to get to their destination or it could be nowhere in a hurry at all. The streets are full of new vehicles, heavy duty double axel work trucks, cars, some looking like they're in the game, others remaining plain with the factory glow. I'm itching to ask my first trick to break the ice and remove the chills from my spine. Being on the road is totally new for me.

Turk suggested we stop by the waffle house to eat breakfast before riding over to Bridge City to work that area first. He decided I would ride with him while Jeff and Rodney paired off to work together. This is how it is usually done, in pairs. Every now and then we'll ride alone but for the most part it's good to keep somebody with you and plus it helps sometimes with the cap game coming from all angles. Bridge City is a couple of miles east of Port Arthur. To get there you have to cross this imitation Golden Gate bridge maybe 2 miles long that drops you into a city at the foot of it that has yet to be crime ridden. The bridge is how the city gets its name. By the look of this city everything may be alright due to the amount of businesses I see that has me calculating the number of doors available that we can enter trying to find a trick. You can smell money by the newness of the buildings and the look of fresh paint. This just might be a gold mine of Texas tea, black gold.

Chapter 5

The Texas heat is assuring you at 8:00am in the morning that it's here and you need to do whatever it is you have to do before midday or it will be too hot. You can feel the heat when you take a breath knowing this is going to be a hot dry day. Our main objective is finding one of these prosperous looking business strips and get down with asking different owners in the hope of catching a good trick and be back at the hotel before lunch lying under the air condition while drinking a cold beer. We usually do this while discussing the last play and how to improve it on the next trick. Playa's say on the road, if you're going to work that hard and long of a day then you need to head back home and get you a 9 to 5 job. Just leave the slum game to real money-getting playa's that's on a mission to drain one of these tricks, and their city, for all its worth. Either be able to con and play for some paper or get out of the way.

This game is not as simple as it sounds because I know plenty of dudes who have tried to sell it but couldn't for one reason or the other - whether it was because of the mental block of not being able to remove the fact that we've just paid $11.75 for a watch that the asking price was $1,000, or the fact that they couldn't make the trick feel them. You have to be able to take the tricks' soul and intertwine it until you're able to lead them by the hand to a place they won't realize they've been until it's too late. By then you're paid and nowhere to be found. Remember without the tricks' greed no con will work. People usually want something for nothing and that is what gets them every time.

We immediately start the process of pulling in and out of business establishments commonly referred to by us as "joints". Turk dropped me off while he pulled further down so we can each start on opposite sides of the strip and meet back up in the middle. Or the first one that makes it back to the car will ride and scout for the other because only one of three things could have happened, or is going on, that sends you straight back to the car. One, you're paid and ready to clear the area. Two, the joints have recently been worked or hit and the tricks are not about to spend any money. Or three, you have a potential trick down and they have spent some money with you and you need to find your partner so he can get a piece of this trick and the both of you can ride out for the day paid in full.

It doesn't take long to determine if a trick is about to pay. If I ask the boss, whether male or female, if they can do anything with it and they say no, I might spit another short line or just move on to the next door while telling them to have a nice day and that I'm only selling costume jewelry from business to business. Often business owners will still call the police to have you checked out. They would call the police station saying guys are riding and walking up and down the streets trying to sell some jewelry that they can't determine if it's real or not. Owners will come all the way out their door and watch you walk down the street trying to see what direction and other businesses you enter which could blow your next trick. This lets the police know what business you're in if they decided they want to talk to you.

About an hour into our flat-footing and walking in and out of doors, I enter into this carpet joint and I'm immediately confronted by this lady who looks to be in her early or mid forties and wealthy. But it's hard to tell white peoples age by sight. I can see a million thoughts running across her forehead. She's wondering if I'm about to rob her or what and I'm thinking to myself, woman I'm about to rob you but not with a pistol. I'll use nothing but conversation. She's trembling as I ask if the boss is in. With her voice barely audible, she responded that she is the boss and can she help me? I flip the jewelry tray open revealing two replica Omega watches, one ladies and one mans, both stamped 14kt on the back. Then I began to spit the game using that famous line I've rehearsed so much that I say it in my sleep and in the dreams I have of stripping these tricks of their money.

"Boss lady can you do anything with these? It's just a ladies and mans Omega watch and I'm not asking that much for them and they aren't local or out of nobody's house." Now everybody knows that the first thing that comes to a white persons mind when seeing a young black male with a tray of shining jewelry is that either he stole it or rob somebody for it. When in reality I've ordered these pieces of jewelry from a reputable slum-house and some of us, such as myself, have never stolen a day in our life not even a pencil in school. This narrow minded way of thinking is what causes tricks to be vulnerable enough to place themselves in a state of mind to be tricked or taken for their bank roll.

This type of mentality is played out all the way to the bus stop by slummers. There's one thing for sure, if there is no greed or larceny in the heart, no matter what sort of merchandise or deal you offer, the individual will not buy. This capitalist society has us basing our self-worth on material items such as homes, automobiles, jewelry and clothes instead of morals, solid principles and character. That's ok with me because without this concept and simple minded way of thinking, I couldn't eat with this game called slumming.

"What you got there?" asked the boss lady.

Now she speaks with great authority in her voice because she's figured out and realized I'm here to offer something as opposed to taking from her. The tone in her voice is as if I'm some low-life scum that should have never been born. But at the same time she's curious as to what I have in the tray and wondering if she could buy it and get away without anybody but her conscious knowing about the leap she's about to take. Now you tell me; what makes this trick any better than me? That's right – nothing, because we both see a win/win situation in our minds and seek to seize upon the opportunity. The only difference is one will win more than the other.

I continue on with Boss Lady, "I brought this to town with me and I'm a long ways from home. Me and your business, Boss Lady, isn't everybody business and you can see right here on my driver's license, Boss Lady that I'm from Mississippi."

Some people try to get proper when talking to white people but, not me. It's best sometimes not to in this game and to let them think you're uneducated and unworthy of society. The game we're playing requires and works best when I revert back to my Mississippi roots as a southern country boy and play the fool she thinks I am.

"What you want for it son?" says the Boss Lady.

"I'll take 15 for it Boss."

"15 what son?" she asked.

"Boss Lady," I said, "You know what I'm talking about and like I said me and your business isn't everybody's business."

"I'll tell you what son," She said, "I'll give you $300.00."

"Boss lady, you're trying to get it the way I got it. The best I can probably do is come get you tonight and when I jump the fence, you can jump it also and get what you're going to get so you won't be trying to rob me for mines Boss Lady. Because for $300.00 Boss Lady, you'll be robbing me without a pistol." You take the script a little deeper only when you know they're not cops or trying to trap you being nosey.

Right about this moment Turk walks in on me and the boss lady. I tell Turk she offered me $300.00 for the tray after I had asked her for $1,500.00 and she said the $300.00 was all she had.

"Hold up and let me talk to her," said Turk.

Now I'm standing here praying to God she don't change her mind before I could get my first piece of money on the road. I really need this lick so I can begin stacking up some money to send back home to Venus and L'il Tony and then I can relax and let it flow like it's going to come. So I'm sitting there fidgeting and tell Turk in a trembling voice that I got this, let me have it. I want to get this little change and flee the scene before the trick decides she don't want anything. Being the inexperienced road slummer that I am at the time, I had yet to perfect the skill of milking tricks for everything and making sure that when one of them said that was all they had, that it was the honest truth.

I hesitated, but stepped back reluctantly, while Turk laid his cap game down on this trick so hard that not only did the trick give me the $300.00 she has offered, but Turk drained her for $1,700.00 more with her lying self saying $300.00 was all she had. The trick couldn't look me straight in the eyes when Turk finished her. I was laughing like crazy at her because she was lying and at the same time getting the experience of her life.

It wasn't that I didn't trust Turk or his ability to work this trick because I've seen his work plenty of times; it was the pressure of being on the road with hotel fair to pay, eating, smoking weed and the need to have my own money to place an order for my own jewelry that had me fidgeting. I had left the house with only a couple of dollars to be able to buy the things I desired to eat and kind of pay my own way as much as possible.

We jetted the tricks' spot(place of business) while watching her stare out the store window as we pulled off in the yellow and black 73 dodge dart that we called a work car/bucket. Turk purchased this automobile especially for this journey. We're now on our way in the opposite direction toward the imitation Golden Gate Bridge back to Port Arthur. Our spirits are high and I'm feeling confident that the road slumming is what I'll be doing from here on out. The thought of selling another grain of weed or the around-town hustling is out of my mind.

On the way back to the hotel room we stopped on the blocks and grabbed us a couple of sacks to smoke and a six-pack of beer and planned on sitting around shooting the breeze and unwinding while discussing the day's events and what we thought was funny about the tricks everybody had caught that day. This always helped you to improve your cap game or use some of each other's cap with a twist. This was a profession and we carried it that way.

Chapter 6

There are always new approaches coming into mind to try on different tricks or the old ones that think they know the game to some degree. Ways you might think won't work will work and that's how it is most of the time. It's the unbelievable that catches them. The cap game is nothing but the ability to come out of your mouth with words in a way that's convincing in order to get the trick to either buy what you're selling or to help push them over the edge for your partner to get paid and out of the way so that you can work on the trick and try to get paid.

Being the newest member of the road crew I take the most getting laughed at about the way I work my tricks and being in a hurry to get out of their offices after getting a small amount of money instead of staying and working them for all I can. Not being the club type of person I hang around the room with Rodney and Jeff this night while Turk decided to hit the club scene. Clubbing has never been my favorite pass-time. Give me a joint, some beer and a little music and I can sit around the house and enjoy that atmosphere just as much as I could any club. Rodney and Jeff's room is a couple doors down from mine and Turk's and I guess after last night's ride to get here and today's working in this heat, they decided not to visit the club scene either. This is not usually a normal thing for either Rodney or Jeff because these two practically live for partying but the Sleep God has other plans for them tonight. About 2:00 in the morning, out of a dead sleep, I hear the sound of Bam! Bam! Bam! with somebody beating on the door as if they're trying to take it off the hinges. This scared me nearly to death. The first thing I do is call their room and Rodney started to cussing telling me to open the door we thought you was dead in there, we've been calling for the last 15 minutes.

When I opened the door Jeff rushed in screaming, "Pack everything up we have to get out of this hotel. Sabrina called and said that trick you caught today in Bridge City screamed and gave a description of the car, and Turk and you to the police and Turk is in Jail. They're looking for the short light-complexioned guy that was with him. The police spotted the car in front of the club and waited for Turk to come out."

My heart is now beating like a drum. I'm so nervous that I catch diarrhea. All kinds of different thoughts and second thoughts are going through my mind about this road game and one of those thoughts is that maybe this game isn't for me after all. I could have stayed home and took a chance of going to jail in a city and area I'm familiar with.

My first time on the road and this has to happen before I can get any kind of bank roll worth talking about and it's all because of my first and only trick since I made it to Texas. I'm now seeing the flip side of the Slum game. Jeff and Rodney are laughing and it's not bothering them the way it's affecting me because they understand how this situation has to play out with simply the returning of the money. I, on the other hand have never seen this side of the game nor been to jail in my life. All I can think is, "What have I gotten myself involved in?"

This is the early 80's and I didn't know that Pepto-Bismol came in tablet form. I'm so nervous about all the drama that's going on around me and the fact that these white folks are looking for a short light-complexioned black male that the Pepto-Bismol's are disappearing fast. I can't be seen because without a doubt they're going to arrest me and take me down town to Port Arthur jail with Turk. At this point I have no idea what the consequences are.

Jeff and Rodney dropped me off at another hotel room. More game now has to be played to raise Turk from jail without a case. Jeff decided he would ride over and speak with the chief of police and play the role of Turk's brother that has recently flew to town with the victims' money and that he has told his brother over and over again about this crap and that he needs to get a job and get his life together.

Jeff was basically feeding the chief a bunch of game to ease the tension surrounding the fact that a white woman in this predominately white city who had been slicked and tricked by some out-of-towner slick black Negro's. The chief placed strong emphasis to Jeff that when Turk is released to not stop him anywhere in this county or surrounding area until he's 100's of miles away from here and not to ever return. If he does, he will personally see to it that he's never let out free again and does he make himself clear?

The money is returned and the police station in Port Arthur is notified to release the master of the game, Turk. The officials have made it clear that they don't want us here playing our con-game on their citizens. Like Coast Playa's, we sought other territory and loaded up similar to the Beverly Hillbillies and headed west in the direction of Houston, Texas, H-Town in search of more black gold, Texas tea.

Antonio Berry

Chapter 7

If you have never been to H-Town or heard about its culture, let me tell you, it's all that and some. As soon as we hit the city in the vicinity of South Main St, you can feel and see success. We continue to ride on and exit seeking the Travel lodge Hotel where other slummers known to us are docked and awaiting our arrival. There are prostitutes and prostitutes everywhere up and down this strip all the way around the bend on Old Spanish Trail doing what they do for a living and for their pimps. I can't believe what my eyes are seeing, and that's this activity is going on so openly and allowed to move freely as if it is legal. Pimps and pimps whips are cruising checking their traps and making sure that their broads are working and never sleeping on the job until their quota is met. What's more unbelievable is, this strip resembles any upper class neighbor-hood in any American city where you may see not only black kids playing together but white and black kids hanging out whose parents are either owners or employees of a fortune 500 company. This scene has me mesmerized because I'm used to seeing this type of activity in the ghetto of the hood.

Its dusk-dark with a still wind and the smell of the city buses diesel fumes permeates the air as they pull from one short stop to the next picking up and dropping off passengers trying to reach their destination. Take my word you can believe what they say about these Cowboys, Oilers and Cow Gangsterette's in Texas. They live by a system and concept that's so engraved in their way of life until it seems fictional. Texans believe in having everything huge, big money, mansion homes, exotic automobiles and big hats. You can taste money here in Houston, Texas. Even when you belch you know that it's here.

Houston is the largest city I've been to outside of Miami, New Orleans and Atlanta. Houston is a city where it's almost impossible to determine which direction is down-town because everywhere you turn there's sky-scrapers reaching the clouds with mirror reflection window panes that gives the impression of magnifying the sun much more than the 95 degree temperature that's being felt.

As we pulled into the Travel Lodge Hotel I noticed all the different out-of-state tags. Turk hit the pimp blow bump bump bump bump four to six quick pecks on the horn. The oldest of the group Doc was from Ohio, Pig Handle Slim and his son Josea and Sweething are from Alabama, Fat Melvin from Detroit, Jimmy and son Bo is from Atlanta, Old Man Shorty Ga is from Atlanta, Mickey, Chuck and Chuck broad Slim Goodie, Chico are all from the Pascagoula area. Chuck use to ride Slim Goodie with him on the road in and out of different states to work the strips same as other prostitutes. Chuck had considered himself a somewhat pimp unable to fall in love and wore his perm to represent. All of them came to their hotel doors at the same time recognizing that international blow of the horn. Greetings are passed around to welcome four more slummers one that's a Jit, myself that has landed in this great big city to drag it for what it's been holding back.

The older playa's that's mentioned had a major hand in grooming my slumming skills and initiated my aka of Bro-n-law. At the end of every workday we all would meet back at the rooms and discuss the day's events as normal and speak on who came up with what kind of lick and somebody always ask Turk, Hey Turk, what did Bro-n-Law do today and the name Bro-n-Law stuck from there. It may have been 9, sometimes 10, cars a morning pulling out of the hotel in search of a good trick and $20,000.00 to $30,000.00 a day may come back in. I was siphoning up all the game I could from these veteran slum playa's and asking any and all questions that came to mind that had me curious about the slum game.

One day while talking to Doc and trying to get a feel for how long this game has been played in such a manner, he broke it down for me. Doc had been slumming since the 50's and this was his life. "

"So Doc, is this the first time you slummed Houston?" I asked him.

Doc said, "No."

"Well how could you come back and it still be as sweet, or sweeter, than before," I asked.

"Because businesses are always closing and new ones' opening. The children may have the business now that their parents once owned. The parents could have once been good tricks and for whatever reason, whether embarrassment or just wanting the children to learn from experience, never pulled their children's coat tail about this game. It could have been their conscious or not wanting the police or anybody else such as friends to be made aware that they would buy stolen items. So now when we go in the place of business after years have passed the game is new to the new owners and plus it was in the late 60's and early 70's when we was last here in Houston and that's how and why the game will always continue to rotate and survive."

This was Doc revelation to me. As long as you continue to only sell from business to business you will always be able to be in the business of slumming and getting money this way on the road. Doc made this clear and he was in front of me as living proof.

I'm now having more money than I've ever had in my life and feeling that I'm a bona fide road hustler and can run with the big dogs. $500.00 to $600.00 a day was a slow day but I can sense things are finally improving and my life is about to change in a major way. I'm hungry for this game and everybody thinks I have great potential to become one of the masters of this game selling watches, rings and chains and any other slum pieces available for me to off. The fellows love having me around and being the youngest of the crew my coat tail is constantly being pulled and asked to come ride. The veterans see themselves in me once upon a time and feel good about passing the game on down to the next generation of could-be great slummers.

I'm constantly being enlightened concerning a better way to perfect the game while avoiding a case, to the history of the slum game and its reward. The rewards can be a big money score to sexing a corporate maybe married broad for a ring, chain or watch and leaving her in distress when she discover that she sold her soul for $1.50 to $15.00 and not the $5,000.00 or $7,000.00 she thought a young brother was giving her for sex. This happened more often than you probably could imagine. There are many female business owners that has tricked/sexed for slum jewelry and they know who they are. It came with the game.

The Beaumont/Port Arthur incident is a forgotten episode never thought about again and behind me. I'm seeing better days and moving up like the Jefferson's. Spending plenty of dough, sending money home, tricking with call girls, the whole nine yards. We commonly ride around Texas Southern University campus trying to trap a female or two. It's 1983 and Hakeem Olajuwon has just signed with the Houston Rockets and we're seeing him on the regular because he also is riding around the university campus in his snow white Eldorado Cadillac macking with the females on campus. The college sits directly across from a project home and has the look of a real hood in the school area.

Chapter 8

Houston was very good to me, as a matter of fact, so good and sweet that it scared the hell out of me. Not the city itself but the money it was coughing up. Jeff and I leave Houston supposedly for the weekend and head in the direction of Mississippi to enjoy the fruits of our labor. We're always welcome by a crowd that viewed us as local celebrities. We did and live with enjoying life better than most dope boys. The plan was to just stay for the weekend but we ended up staying until our money had begin to look funny and instead of going back to Houston where we knew it was a gold mine, I let Jeff convince me to try Baton Rouge, Louisiana. I did not have a clue that in the back of Jeff's mind he only wanted to keep an eye on his broad Monae that was attending college at Southern University.

We laid in Baton Rouge and dragged the city until it wouldn't produce nothing else and it became so hard that we was forced to try and catch moving tricks or tricks coming out of stores in order to eat and pay motel rent. We had actually gone from going inside of businesses to riding around flashing our trays at passing automobiles and automobiles stopped at red lights. This was going backward and a low grade of slumming and a black eye to the game as for the way we was given it all in the name of Jeff trying to work and watch his broad. No man will ever be able to work and watch his woman at the same time. There's two things hated by real playa's, a begging woman and a crying man.

The hustling Jeff had us doing wasn't going anywhere and being a rookie I was still easy to influenced by the fun of the game but I knew this wasn't the feeling I was having in Texas; nor the money. All we were able to do is pay rent at the motel and re-order more slum to work and sometimes less slum than we had sold or what our prior order had added up to be. We was going downhill and going down fast. We was repeating a bad cycle day in and day out and this wasn't panning out for me because I had mouths to feed at home who depended on me for some sort of support.

Jeff had a few dollars in the bank there in Baton Rouge and was now spending it faster than we could make it. He was trying to stick it out just to keep an eye on Monae. He continued trying to convince me that it was going to get better. One day I woke up on the wrong side of the bed and said this is it I'm going home and try to get myself together so I can try this again. This didn't set too well with Jeff and we almost fought about the idea of leaving and I didn't care because I was refusing to be broke or continue to hustle backward.

I said, "Fool I have a family and child to feed, I'm lucky Venus was working and able to help hold it down at the house while I'm out here doing nothing with this mess you have us doing. We're not stacking any money and I haven't sent any home in almost a month." So I tell him, "You can stay here Jeff but I'm gone."

Back at the house I contacted one of my old school partners named Snap and ran the situation down to him and what had happened. Snap also knew the slum game but had yet to take that leap on the road. We both are sitting around the house brain storming on a plan. We have little money and, truth be told, we were broke as hell.

Then it hit me, ring, ring, ring. "Hello," said my brother Darryl when he answered my Mom's phone.

"What's up?" I asked.

"Nothing," stated Darryl.

"Where's Mama?" I asked.

"She's in the kitchen," said Darryl.

"Put her on the phone. Mama I need a favor," I said to her.

"What is it now Tony?" She asked.

"I need to borrow some money," I asked.

Mama snapped, "What kind of money Tony?"

"I need $500.00 and I'll pay you back in a couple of weeks," I told her.

"I knew this was coming. What do you need with this much money?" asked Mama. And she went on to tell me that I need to get my butt a job, start staying home and stop whatever it is I'm doing. All that running around from here to there and for what?

"Are you going to let me borrow the money or not?" I replied. Because now I'm heated and I'm not trying to hear what she's saying or listen to a lecture.

"I got this bank book of yours you had when you was in school come get it and when it's gone don't come to me again," she said.

I had totally forgotten about that bank account. I had been saving money since back in the days when I use to help my grand-daddy at his place of businesses.

All I'm thinking or could think now was, "I have to make this work and stay on top of my game and never fall again." A job was something I didn't see as an option for me - not after tasting the blood of the slum game and life on the road.

It's November 1983 and Snap and I decided to hit the road together without Jeff this time because our relationship has been seriously damaged because of his weakness for a broad. Snap and I both are hoping to have a sweet and blessed holiday season.

Jeff is now going in a separate direction and not really wanting to be bothered with us, he's deep in his feelings because we refused to hang around in Baton Rouge. He tried to tell Snap his side but Snap couldn't get through to him either to make him see the wrong in how he was thinking. It was all good because I didn't chase my own woman and sure as hell wasn't going to follow another man chasing his.

Snap and I was now on our way to becoming professional Slummers and plan on getting it right this time. We're riding like crazy from state to state, city to city: Texas, Oklahoma, Kansas, New Mexico. The money is rolling in and at the end of every week we at least try to send anywhere from $1,500.00 to $2,000.00 home to save for when we come off the road. December is approaching and fast. Venus is due with our second baby any day. I'm trying but it don't seem like I'm going to make it in time to witness her give birth to the newest addition to our family.

Chapter 9

There is this town in North Texas named Sherman that I will never forget; or the friends Snap and I met there. Snap and I are cruising down the main drag after a day's work and having come up pretty decent with a bank roll for it to be our first day in town, plus we started late in the day. We're riding searching for the local hood to purchase our favorite pass time, a bag to smoke. The sun has just begun to hide itself on the West Coast.

"Snap, check out that red bone in that Toyota next to us," I said. "I'm going to flash this tray on her and see if she bites."

I had to take a double look at this Goddess. Regardless of how good and sexy a broad was, I would never take my eyes off the prize of getting paid because I was definitely about my money.

Being a young brother with a thirst for Ben Franklins, I flashed the tray on this Red Bone and her eyes widened so fast that it surprised me. She pointed her finger for me to pull over in the direction of the shopping center parking lot of the plaza to the right of us. I pulled over and hopped out and walked over to Red's driver-side window in hopes of catching a good look at some thighs. I could not stop staring into those grayish eyes while at the same time she's being mesmerized by the glitter in the jewelry tray. She lifts up the lady's watch turning it over in her hand and asked how much? Sympathy is a counterfeit mood for suckers so I politely ask her for $500.00 and while she's flipping this figure over in her mind, I'm thinking of a cap game to get paid and a way to see her again without putting myself or Snap in danger of any drama.

The clothes she has folded in baskets in the back seat of her car gives me the impression that she's coming from the Laundromat.

"All I have is $100.00," Red said.

I give her a simple basic reply, "I wish I was able to give it to you, because for $100.00 that's just what I'll be doing, giving it away."

After going back and forth for a couple of minutes and getting a good feel for one another's spirits I say, "Tell you what, give me the $100.00 and come by the hotel where I'm staying and let me treat you to dinner." Now this is where a brother might be slipping and starting to think with his little head. I know too well that this trick broad will be coming back for her money as soon as she wakes up to the fact that she has been had and tricked.

"That broad was pretty and fine as hell," said Snap.

We continued on to the block to buy some weed and then headed back in the direction of the room to relax and work up an appetite on the Mexican-grade weed and cold beer.

I was hoping that Red would show up and couldn't get her off my mind. I only hope she don't bring the police or any other type of drama when she comes. But I know she'll be coming to check if I gave her a valid address. About an hour had passed before Snap and I are good and hungry and feeling the pain of needing something to eat. We head in the direction to get something solid to put on our stomach for tonight because we probably won't come back out until in the morning. And that would be for breakfast.

As soon as Snap opened the door he stepped back in quickly and said, "She's out there Bro-n-Law and she is blocking your car."

"Ok, let me step out and holla at her and see what's on her mind," I said.

When I came to the door, Red was sitting there long-faced, motioning with her finger for me to come towards her car.

You have to be careful in this type of situation because the trick could be so hurt and embarrassed that she might have come to kill. I'm cautiously watching my surroundings while approaching her car. My mind is running 100 mph in all directions wondering how this situation is about to play itself out.

Just as I reached Red's car, she says in a sexy, sultry, pitiful whisper, as if that was necessary, that she wanted her money back. This immediately sends me in a cap game mood, especially now that I know everything is under control as long as I play my cards right.

"Check this out Red. I'm going to give you your money back, you can keep the watch, and I'm going to treat you to dinner," I told her.

She's trying to speak but I keep stopping her in mid-sentence.

"Hold it, let me explain. I never wanted your money, it was you I wanted to see again and if that's not true I would have never told you where I was living to come ask for it back. So think about it. I'm only happy that you didn't bring the police or the drama that you could have came with to ask for it back and I'm damn happy that you came."

She smiled and the tension quickly eased and took a turn for the best.

Chapter 10

"Red, my name is Tony and I'm from Mississippi and this is what I do for a living, ride state to state, City to City putting this game down what you just experienced firsthand for a living, it's my livelihood. I love what I'm doing and doing what I love and you tasted it so you need no convincing that it works and gets me paid. My partner and I were in the process of going to Piccadilly to get a bite to eat why don't you follow and dinner is on me." This is where our relationship began, if you can call it a relationship because it wasn't the usual man/woman relationship.

Snap, is my road-dawg. He's dark complexioned 5'9, 165 lb and cool as an ice cube. He's as smooth as they come. We have been tight since Colmer Junior High School. Snap grew up in Carver Village and has seen Playa's come and go.

To this day we still communicate one way or the other whether it's direct or through mutual friends and family. Red introduced Snap to one of her friend girls who was just as jet black as Snap was and we nick-named her Blacky. At the time I did know their government names but have long forgotten them. Red and Blacky came by every morning to check on us whenever they hadn't laid around the room all night spending time with us watching a movie or just sitting around talking. The truth is they had eased up under us so brilliantly we had even given them a key to the room. We would leave money for them so they could already have some weed for us when we got in from working. Sometimes they would have us a hot meal waiting or would have taken our clothes to the cleaners if needed.

While lying around watching television Red and I would wrestle on the bed and enjoy the moment as if we had known each other for a life time. Snap and his girl would do the same but the difference was Snap and his girl had gotten close enough to where they felt comfortable having sex. Red and I would leave the room to go to the store and as soon as we walk back in the door you could see the guilt and passion on their faces. Red is dragging me and has yet to give it up. For the life of me I can't figure out why she will not have sex with me.

Red would not give me the booty and kept giving me the same excuse and story line about she didn't want to get her heart broken and she thought it was best we take it slow. Red was looking for a long term relationship and would always make the statement that she wanted to see how long I'll be around and didn't want to be anybody's one night stand. This was not happening in my mind-set at the time. It was always hit 'em and leave them in whatever state or city it may be.

One day out of the presence of Red I asked Blacky, "Why is Red tripping and giving a Brother such a hard time about having Sex?"

Blacky said, "Listen Tony, I don't know what or how you told her what you did to sell her that watch but it messed up the trust issue for now because of the way you were able to get in her mind and lead her in the direction you did. It was scary to her that somebody she didn't even know was able to trap her like that and then look how smooth you did it to make sure you seen her again. She likes you a lot and thinks you're good people regardless of that because you explained it to her and showed her you don't do everybody that way. You're still going to have to take it slow with her and let time take its course. She's afraid to wake up one morning after and you're a distant past to never be seen again."

"Blacky I do what I do and this is what I do for a living," I replied.

That's exactly what happened after about three to four weeks of lying around Sherman, Texas and hadn't knocked Red off. Snap and I woke up in the middle of the night with a vision and rode out with the sun in the direction of Oklahoma.

Red and Blacky hadn't laid over that night. We never heard of them again and had nothing to remember them by except that they both was good people and showed us wonderful hospitality while in their city. In light of me not getting the booty from Red I enjoyed the time spent with her.

Antonio Berry

Chapter 11

Red was absolutely correct, I had no intentions of hanging around because the only thing I was in love with was roaming the country side selling rings, chains and watches while enjoying the view and thinking about my next trick that's hiding somewhere in the crevices of sweet America.

Snap and I worked Oklahoma City and the surrounding area for several weeks until we had figured it was enough damage done. On the way there I had gone to jail for a traffic violation in the City of Muskogee and now they have paid dearly....

Oklahoma was, as they say, Ok and we did fairly well there with the catching of tricks from $500.00 to $1,500 a day. Don't get it twisted because there were some days in these cities we didn't make a dime. The landscape was very beautiful and something you may see in the National Geograpic magazine picturing the sunset closing its eyes to this side of the world.

The Federal Office Building that was bombed on April 19,1995 was the building that housed the Comptroller's Office where Snap and I had to go to get a tax ID number before being able to get a city license to sell from business to business.

The entire time we were working Oklahoma we had our minds on Albuquerque, New Mexico. The location on the map made it look, promising and secluded from the slum game and the Coast Playa's. We would always try and send money home each week until we get there which sometimes would be months and especially when leaving a spot because you didn't have to worry about running upon a trick and giving the money back. We're definitely leaving this state.

Before we made our way toward 1-40, we detoured and stopped at the local Western Union to do our usual thing of sending money home whenever we're done with a city or pulling out for whatever reason. Whether it's because the tricks are not biting anymore, the police run us out or we have just hit a good lick and have no intentions of giving anything back. We never send money home until we are completely through with a city.

Chapter 12

New Mexico was a beautiful state and we had even seen a balloon festival that was part of the state's tradition. It was the first balloon festival either of us had ever seen.

We arrived in Albuquerque in a winter month. The snow would be falling in one part of the city on East Central towards the mountains and 1-40 exit, while on the other end towards downtown and The University of New Mexico, the sun would be shining.

Between downtown and the end of Central Street, students would be hanging out in the local area pubs, book stores and restaurants. The motel we docked at was on East Central towards 1-40 where the snow was falling. The weed we copped in the Mexican hood was some of the best we had smoked in a while and it was green and plentiful.

The first few days there this broad began to sweat us but little did she know what or who she was about to get tangled with. Every day after work Snap and I would ride through the Mexican's block to get us a sack or just cruising checking out the way they had their cars hooked up. One day this healthy Mexican/black mixed broad confronted us about who we were and where we was from and the conversation took a life of its own with Snap looking at me as if what's up? So we told her to get in.

As we're turning a few corners taking the long way back to the motel we're also trying to get this broad as full of liquor as we can so the understanding of what we had on our mind wouldn't be hard to understand. The broad is smoking our weed drinking our beer as if she's down with whatever. Around 8:00 pm the three of us are as high as the sky, eyes beaming like head lights and a brother is full of lust. I cracked the broad about getting naked and she rebelled and say she don't get down like that, ain't no train going to be ran on her. She's talking real crazy as if she thought she was going to just do one of us and not the other - bad move on her part. Now she is beginning to realize what it is and the type of brothers she has voluntarily got involved with. Since she has started to act a fool the best sleep she's going to get was in a chair until she gets dropped off the next morning. That's what she got - a bad night's sleep in a chair.

It's January, 1984 and after working Albuquerque and the surrounding cities of Santé Fe, and Socorro. Snap and I had the urge to head back towards Mississippi to relax and reminisce on the first successful experience we'd had on the road all on our own. We were going home to the family to enjoy the fruits of our labor and for me to see my new born girl Antrice.

Chapter 13

After a couple of months of touring the country, Venus and I are having some serious ups and downs in our relationship and there are more downs than ups. She's not happy with me always being on the road when she would rather I had a 9-to-5 job with benefits that would allow me to spend more time with her and L'il Tony and new born baby girl Ms. Ann. This type of talking is the very reason I find it easy to stay gone and on the road the extended time that I do. I do not want to hear about getting a job and all the in-love fantasy she's having. Bills have to be paid, food on the table, clothes on the children's backs and love will not do all those things, not for me anyway. I'm still wrestling with the question of maybe having another child whose mother insists that I'm not the father.

I can remember this conversation Venus and I had one day while I was on the road and calling home to check on her and the children. Venus mentioned something about her mother stating that the school district was hiring and she wanted me to come home and check on it to see if I could get employed.

I calmly and politely asked, "Did you pick up the money I sent you through western union yesterday?"

"Yes," Venus answered.

"Are the bills paid?" I asked.

"Yes, the bills are paid Tony," answered Venus.

"Is your car giving you any problems?" I asked.

"No," Venus answered.

"What about the children, they're not sick or out of diapers and milk are they?" I asked.

"No, and why are you asking all these questions Tony, and not answering me about what my mama said about the school district?" She asked.

"I'll tell you what Venus. This is what you do for me. Call your Mom and tell her thanks and for her to take the job," and I hung up on her.

I wasn't trying to hear anything remotely close to or about getting a job and wasn't looking for one. I had finally begun to see myself having real dope money in the slum game for the first time and started to wonder if Venus was crazy or stupid and was hoping she wouldn't make me choose between her and the game that I'm loving because she would lose. There had been moments when we barely had money to pay the bills and buy groceries. I'd cop a quarter or half pound of weed to flip some money and buy groceries without being broke and staying afloat. There's no way, my mind was made up to let her go before I let this slum game I'm eating on drop by the way-side. The game is being too good to me to turn my back on it.

Chapter 14

While lying around the house one night playing with Man and Ms. Ann, Kango, out of the blue, called and said, "What's up Bro-n-law?"

"I'm just chillin spending time with the kids," I replied.

"I got somebody I want you to meet," said Kango, "Ride down to Pascagoula and call me at this number when you get in the area."

Kango knew Venus and I was having some serious relationship problems because of the aggravation she was causing me about being on the road. I got up and headed in the direction of Pascagoula to meet Kango. He introduced me to Janice and that was the beginning of our relationship.

Janice was brown complexioned with long black hair, 5'5", 130 lbs with full lips and a big pretty smile and very feminine. I immediately fell in love with her and knew that if I wasn't careful at this vulnerable time in my life especially when things are falling apart at home that this could have a devastating effect on my marriage. With this belief in mind, I played it real careful and by ear but continue to see Janice on the low after we were introduced. We were enjoying the time spent together whenever time permitted. In the mean time Snap and I were planning our next trip.

I pulled out the atlas and begin to study what state and route may be good for us to take in pursuit of a bank roll and decided on the Sunshine state of Florida, the first city was going to be Orlando.

Orlando was sweet. Our first night was spent sleeping on Orange Blossom Trail (OBT). OBT is one of the main strips of tourist attraction. There's peep shows, clubs, restaurants, arcades, prostitutes, motels and many businesses along this miles and miles of high-density-traffic road. There's even one club that has an airplane hanging from inside the building simulating the plane crashing into the building.

In three weeks we had ants in our pants and were ready to move further. The weather was very good and sunny days were common here in Florida. We set our sights on the west coast of Florida, St. Petersburg, in Pinellas County. It was just as we thought, sweet and full of tricks.

The entire side up and down Hwy 19 from St. Pete to New Port Richey was nothing but businesses for us to enter in and out of trying to find a good trick with greed in their hearts to take some of this slum off our hands for a small fee.

Everything that glitters is not gold and these tricks on this side of the country had never seen the game played like this before and especially by a black man with enough nerve to enter their place of business with a tray of jewelry to sell to the boss. If they had seen it on this side of the state, it had to have been a long time ago because 95% of the businesses acted like it was their first time to encounter this kind of game.

Ignoring everybody at the front door or desk, I'm looking for the person with the check book and the keys to that big-body Benz parked out-side. If any of the front desk people or employees get in my business and gets caught up being nosey and trying to wake the boss up and get all in my affairs, which happens on occasions, then they will get it also. Some of them find themselves borrowing money off their check until payday after I've made it clear and told them, the employees, that this is not for them it was only for the boss.

Most of the time it was the Negro employees trying to be nosey and act like they know everything. With the end result being them not able to pay their light bill come next week because they bought something worth nothing. It came from interfering in my business and my means of survival.

During this time we were working out of a brown LTD II I'd purchased just for the purpose of riding the road. Its work, weed block and back to the motel. A brother is on a serious mission when he's on the road from sun up to sun down looking for a trick. Every stop is a play from the convenience stores where we would get $20.00 dollars worth of gas for $10.00 and a double order of fries without salt. Once you tell them you asked for no salt they would pass you another order without requesting the first one back.

Snap and I would sometimes go in the store and immediately pay for the gas with our pump already set. We'll walk around inside the store for a few minutes and then one of us would go to the counter and pay for our items and head outside. Once outside we'd get the other's attention in the store to ask the clerk to turn on the pump. Now they can't remember doing it when we first came in and the both of us have been in the store the entire time and they would reset it. That's how we would get $20.00 dollars worth of gas for $10.00. Every now and then Snap and I would take a local broad back to the room to knock off to keep the cheat off us.

Antonio Berry

Chapter 15

This is our first time working Florida and it's wonderful. The weather is great, the atmosphere is relaxed and everybody seems to be gullible in wanting something for nothing.

On most days we're able to leave for work no later than 8:00 am and be back at the motel, or at least off work, before 12:00 pm with a bank roll of a $1,000 to $1,500.

Four weeks have passed since Snap, my baby brother Darryl and I have come to Florida to work these tricks on this end of the globe. I'm calling Venus and Janice allowing myself to be tortured between the two trying to determine which way and to whom to turn. Venus is in one ear bugging the hell out of me to give up what I'm doing in order to stay home and spend more time with her and the children when she knows I love this road game. She's about to make me choose between her and this game and don't know how close she is to losing. Janice on the other hand wants me to continue to do whatever it is that's making me happy and she could live with just knowing that we're going to spend some time together whenever possible and I'm home off the road.

Janice and I are really feeling one another and all I can do is think about her 24/7 and long for the time to get back there to her. I'm even trying to figure out a way to be back in town three or four days before Venus knows I'm back. I'm trying to think of ways to spend more time with Janice anyway possible and get away without listening to Venus' fussing and arguing. She has an idea that something is going on because I'm no longer paying her any attention about anything she complains about because in the back of my mind she's history and don't know it. She has run me off in another direction when all she had to do was keep her mouth closed and ride the tide while living comfortable. It's not like I wasn't taking care of my business.

It's Friday and we just caught a trick for $3,500 on the St. Pete side of Florida and we'll say lets ride out towards Mississippi for the weekend. Our adrenaline is running like a hyped NFL football player that has won the Super Bowl. As we're traveling North on Hwy 19/41 in the direction of North Florida trying to connect to I-10 west, we're smoking weed and talking trash about all the tricks we caught in the last month while in this state. My baby brother Darryl is with us and we're reminiscing about the good times we've had and listening to Morris Day sing the Oaktree, everybody do the bird. Jerome was my favorite in the band.

As we approached Lake City, Florida the car engine begins to rattle as if the engine is trying to jump from under the hood and we're in the middle of nowhere and its pitch dark. I tell Snap and Darryl that it looks like we're not going to make it. The more I mash the gas, the slower the car begins to role. We passed the first rest area to the right on I-10 you come to once you straighten out heading west towards Tallahassee off 1-75. Its 8:45 pm and the car is losing pressure by the feet, not miles.

About four miles past the rest area the engine shut completely off. The only choice we have is to try and locate a phone, which could be miles away in either direction, and call for some help. We know its 4 to 5 miles behind us but have no idea how far one is in our front direction.

My mind is working overtime on a plan to make this incident pay off like a good lick from a trick. I'm always on the grind. The game don't stop or change, only an added twist when needed and now is one of those times one is needed so here comes the twist. Then it hit me and I knew without a doubt that my plan would work.

Darryl and I make it to a phone about two miles west of us while Snap stayed in the car. Naturally the first person I would call is my wife

Venus whom I thought without a doubt would not hesitate and would break her neck in trying to assist her husband in this dilemma. After about two hours of calling and trying to reach Venus, knowing Snap is wondering what the hell is happening, I finally made contact with her and as soon as she answered the phone the anger I had been holding in for the last two hours seeped out with venom.

"I've been trying to reach you for last past two hours. Where in the hell have you been? Then you have the nerves to talk about I need to stay home and come off the road!" I asked.

Venus stated that her and her friend Darlene had taken the children to the mall and stopped for some pizza. Venus not knowing where all the frustration in my voice is coming from because she knows this is not my usual behavior because I could care less about where she spends her time, especially when I spend mine all over the country. I care more about how she spends my money than I do about her time. It was the fact that I was stranded and was in desperate need of some help and she wasn't available that had me steaming.

"Shut up and listen, we're broke down in the middle of nowhere on I-10 ninety miles east of Tallahassee. We were on our way home when the car engine completely stopped on us and we need somebody to come get us off the side of the road." I told her.

"How do you expect me to do that when you know my car is not highway ready?" replied Venus.

"What the hell do you mean what do I expect you to do?" This is where I lost it. "Bitch, you can get your friends to run you around to the malls and spend the got damn money I'm out here getting, which the situation I find myself in now is a direct result of, but you can't get them to take you to pick up your stranded husband off the side of the highway? Don't worry about it - later!" I hung up on Venus never to feel the same about our relationship again.

The only other person I could think of that came to my mind was Janice and this could be the moment that seals her faith with me and she has no idea that a call is about to be made that will forever change her life. Janice picked the phone up on the third ring and said she was just lying there thinking about me and wondering if she was going to hear from me today or had I forgotten about her, she did not know I was trying to surprise and sneak up on her. Never that I stated, how could I?

"Snap, Darryl and I are in a situation and need some help." I told her.

"Her immediate response was, "What do you need?"

I said, "We're broke down on the highway about ninety miles east of Tallahassee on I-10 and need somebody to come pick us up and we'll pay them."

"Call me back in a few minutes," She replied, "I'm going to call Tweety and whoever I can to see who I can come up with. Give me about thirty minutes," Said Janice, "Just in case I have to really search for somebody, but I'm coming."

 This was the longest thirty minutes of my life but when I finally called back she had taken care of her business and was on her way to get us. Jeff had said he would come. Although we might have our disagreements, Jeff had a heart and he could be counted on in a serious time of need and this couldn't be more serious. He knew that I could be counted on too, if he ever needed me.

I thought, 'What's the difference?' We needed some help no matter where it came from and this might just be the peace offering between Jeff, Snap and myself that we needed. Plus, I had my plan to further get paid from this little incident.

I said, "Alright come on and get us. When are y'all leaving?"

"In a few minutes," said Janice.

Now that's how a broad is supposed to move and get down for her man and she doesn't have an idea about the real effect of what has transpired between the two of us. Venus has allowed herself to get played right out the door and played out of her man.

Darryl and I headed back to the car where Snap had been patiently waiting and probably thinking something has happened to us. We're going to get some sleep and rest while we wait for our rescue. I began to strategize and run it past Snap and Darryl how I'm going to pull this plan off to further get paid from this break down. Six hours later Jeff and Janice, and Janice's cousin Pam, drives up in Jeff's red-orange looking Cheech and Chong van. Everybody gives a round of pounds and greetings and this goes on for a few minutes and I tell Jeff thanks for coming.

"This is what I need to do," I say to Jeff, "I want to push the car to the other side of the interstate and direct it going east so when I get home I'm going to report the car stolen from the mall and collect the insurance like the white folks do. I need to create the scene as if the thief left heading this way."

"Bro-n-law, man you're on the grind for real," said Jeff.

"If it's for the taking without throwing bricks at the penitentiary then I have to have it," I told him.

Janice and I are enjoying what little comfort we can with one another in the back of Jeff's van for the time being. Everybody can see that we're two love birds that are feeling each other's vibes. This is the beginning of a new chapter in both of our lives. Janice is three years and a couple months older than I am but the youngster is putting it down so hard and making life seem so simple and easy, that it's hard for any female to resist the presentation of this young Coast Playa.

Antonio Berry

Chapter 16

On the way home all I can think about was how Venus wouldn't go the extra mile to try and help me and how the woman lying in my arms not only made it happen, but didn't hesitate or pass word back as an excuse to avoid helping me out of the situation I was in.

Janice had missed a day from work and the more I thought about it the more pissed off I became at Venus. Now I'm seriously contemplating ending this poor excuse of a marriage with her. It's bad enough I have to deal with her constantly nagging me about being gone on the road but, now I see I can't really depend on her to have my back when I truly need her. There's no way she's going to continue to enjoy and live off me this way and show no appreciation or loyalty. As for that matter, she has never shown any concern for my welfare.

Lucky for her she's at work when I make it home because I walked in ready to spit venom in her direction. She won't be home for several hours so this gives me time to freshen up and think some more on what has to be done concerning our marriage. There's no doubt it has gone too far and is beyond repair.

As soon as she walked through the door with that happy-grin smile like it's all good, I cut her in half. "I see nothing funny or anything to smile about so I must have missed the joke. We need to talk because I don't think this marriage is working out for us and it makes no sense to stay together if we're not happy."

"So what are you trying to say Tony?" asked Venus.

"I'm not trying to say anything Venus, I'm saying it. I called you to come help me off the side of the interstate broke down in the middle of nowhere and all you did was make excuses as to why you couldn't help me before even making an attempt to help or seeking some help for me. You tell me how I'm suppose to feel about that when I'm riding across country making sure you and the children don't want for nothing and then you pull some foul disloyal shit like that as if I'm nobody to you? What good are you to me then if I can't count on you to have my back?"

"Tony I have two children and a car that is not in the best of shape and I'm doing the best I can while you're running up and down the highway."

Slap! "Don't you ever come out your mouth like that again with me, you ungrateful good-for-nothing bitch. I'm sending you my highway money and you don't complain when you're spending it but now when I needed you, you find excuses not to show some loyalty. I ride across this country looking for tricks and you think I'm going to let you make me feel like one? This is the reason why I've decided to pack my bags and leave!"

From that point on our relationship hasn't been the same and was going downhill faster than a roller coaster. I've begun to stay out all night sometimes until 5:00 am.

On most mornings I have Janice to drop me off a few blocks from the house on her way to work and I walk the rest of the way. On this one particular morning after being dropped off, I walked in the house and Venus is sitting at the kitchen table looking crazy, eyes red as if she has been up all night crying.

I asked her what was up and why was she up that time of morning? She stated she was waiting for me to come home. She said that I needed to go ahead and pack my bags because she wasn't going to live like this and if I didn't want to be there with her and the children then leave but she was not about to put up with this anymore.

I hadn't packed my bags as I originally said I was going to because I truly didn't want to leave my children but I had made up my mind to do whatever gave me a sense of peace. During these days the only thing that was giving me that peace was spending time with Janice.

"What is it that you want me to do Tony?" said Venus, "I've apologized and apologized to you and its nothing more I can do. I try not to think about you choosing the road instead of finding a job. I haven't been on your back about it lately. If there's someplace in the streets you'd rather be than spending time with us when you're home, then 'bye. I'd rather the children and I be alone than to put up with this mess from you. I'm not going to let you run over me and put up with your trifling just because you think you're doing such a good job taking care of us. Don't you forget I work too and held things down for us before it got good for you," stated Venus. She did have a point because there was a time when we were in Baton Rouge that if she hadn't been working it would have been horrible.

Weeks have passed and I've tried to slow down and believe that Venus also knows that I'm serious about getting out of this marriage if she don't allow me to do what I love to do without having to listen to her mouth. And the thing I love is taking this slum game across the country like a Coast Playa.

I actually did slow down a great deal because the truth is I did want to be a father that was there for his children on every turn and to be able to watch them grow up to be teenagers and then adults.

Antonio Berry

Chapter 17

I'm barely seeing Janice and it's hard to get her to understand because she has now gotten me in her system like a bad habit that not only she can't shake but don't want to shake. I've honestly made my mind up to try and keep my family together and actually had a sit-down talk with Venus about us moving to Texas. She's all for it and I'm not sure whether it's because she sees it as a way to get me away from Janice, or because the town was screaming and she was hearing it from the streets or she really did want to move and try for a new start. Maybe she's thinking it will change my behavior? I really don't know but she agreed and that's all that mattered to me at this time.

For the next couple of days we prepared to leave on a journey that would normally take five hours but my idea was for it to take several weeks to get to our destination of Houston, Texas. I had planned to work every city possible along the way. I can't shake Janice from my mind and its killing me but the urge to do the right thing is much greater. Every city except Beaumont, Texas and Baton Rouge, Louisiana will be worked before we arrive in Houston.

We leave and our first stop is New Orleans, eighty to ninety miles from Pascagoula/Moss Point, Mississippi. We docked at a motel on Chef Hwy right below the high-rise bridge. Antrice is still a arms baby and hadn't yet begun to take steps. Li'L Tony is running around wanting to hit the door behind me every time I turn the knob. It's me, Snap, Todd, aka Chicken, Ernest, aka Cat, that's working together.

Chicken and Cat are two of our partners at the time that sometimes would ride local with us. But now we have decided to take them on the road for the first time because they can sell it also and won't be a burden and will be able to pay their way.

Snap and I ride out to work together while Chicken and Cat paired off in two's as a working team of cap buddies. The two cars pulled off from the motel in opposite directions not knowing what lies ahead for the day and having no idea where we will find our tricks to pay us. This is our first time working New Orleans and it is not familiar territory. For several days we work the area and are coming up pretty decent with a bank roll of $600.00 to $800.00 a day so it's looking as if we might be here for a couple of days dragging before continuing on towards Texas. I don't want to leave any business untouched and have no reason or desire to work this city for years to come.

Venus is happy and now feeling very secure about having me all to herself and my effort to keep the marriage together. Little does she know I couldn't keep Janice off my mind no matter how hard I tried I just couldn't shake her or the times we spent together. I'm wrestling with the thought of Houston, Texas and don't know if I'm going to make it. I'm beginning to think it was a bad idea to stop this close to home. I should have continued and not stopped until I crossed the Texas state line.

On this cloudy Thursday morning Snap and I decided to ride over to work a city called Chalmette in St. Bernard Parish with hopes of catching a real good trick in this rich looking area. It looks very rich and well-to-do from the way the homes are structured and the automobiles that being driven.

We're in and out of joints as fast as the boss can say no he can't use it and we move on to the next door. We're nibbling up on $100.00 here $200.00 there, $50.00 for a chain here and there. I walked into this used car lot and asked for the boss not knowing I was talking to him.

"I'm the boss," this pot-bellied, Cajun man said.

"Boss, how you doing?" I ask.

"Can I help you?" asked the boss.

"Yes, I got this lady and man's watch and a few gold chains and I ain't asking that much for them, think you might be able to do anything with them?" I said.

"Let me see what you got there boy," he demanded.

"Just some Omega watches boss, and they ain't local." I told him.

I'm young at this time; only 19 years old to be exact. As boss is being mesmerized by the glitter, I'm pushing the cap game in his ear as hard as I can. Hoping to keep him on the line and praying he bites hard enough for Snap and me to get paid off. The sky has gotten dark and was threatening rain and we wanted this one trick so we could head back to the motel before it started raining. It has definitely gone from being cloudy to now looking as if the bottom is about to fall out of these clouds.

"What do you want for all of it?" said Boss.

"You ain't the police are you boss?" I asked.

"No, I'm not the damn police!" screamed Boss.

"Just had to ask boss before I put you deep in my business; I don't want you being worried thinking this stuff is local or out of somebody's house. It didn't even come out of this state. I brought it across the state line with me when I came. Look right here on my license, I'm from Mississippi and I came here with all this you see." Now nothing I said to boss was a lie.

I tell boss what I'll take for the whole tray of jewelry and watches. As he thinks about this figure in his mind, he asked will I take check.

"Yes, I'll take a check boss but, what I really could use is a car. The one I'm driving is about to stop on me any moment now. You know an even swap ain't no swindle and a fair exchange ain't no robbery boss." I told him.

"You see something you like out there?" asked Boss.

"Yeah, I like that 77 Grand Prix you got out there for $3,500 and boss you know you don't have $3,500 invested and I'd be surprise if you have $1,000 tied in it. So what do you say boss, can we deal or what? I'll tell you what boss, this is the best I'll be able to do without letting you rob and take advantage of me without using a pistol. I'll give you the two $1,200 watches , one $800.00 rope chain and the $400.00 flat herring-bone chain for the car with the title and a couple of hundred of dollars for me to buy some gas to get back home."

"Son, that ain't no deal," said boss, "I'll give you the car with a clean title and tag that's good for two years for everything you have in that jewelry box," he offered.

"Boss you're robbing me without a pistol if I do that. If I do that you have to promise me that if I bring something over here to you next week trying to put some money in my pocket, you have to promise me that you'll going to look out and treat me fair."

"Sure bring it to me," said boss.

I know damn well he's lying and just trying to get me out of there as fast as he can so he could go and hide what he thinks is his deal of the century. He can't wait to get me from around his place of business in case somebody notices something suspicious.

"Ok, you got a deal boss but don't act like you don't know and owe me when I come back and not wanting to give me what I ask for the next time when I have gave you the deal of a life time," I told him.

For two $11.75 watches, one $2.00 rope chain, one $1.50 flat herringbone chain and a jewelry box that cost $3.00. For a total price of about $30.00 I drive off in the rain in a 77 Grand Prix in the direction of New Orleans some 10 miles away to pick up my family so we can go out to get us a bite to eat and for them to see daddy's work. Boss will never forget this little young bright-complexioned Negro with such a big heart. It was a lesson well learned for him by a Coast Playa.

Chapter 18

The thought of Janice is wearing on me heavy and the more I think about having come up with a fat bank roll in a couple of days with another vehicle, Texas don't sound that exciting to me anymore. Texas does not sound exciting enough for me to move there and forget about Janice.

All I have to do now is figure out a way to bring these feelings to Venus. I know this idea and thought is going to cause her to become suspicious and possibly rebel against the idea. It may work or it may not but I'm going to sleep on it for a couple of more days before bringing it to her because she just might act a fool and flip out because her mind is really set on us leaving Mississippi behind in the past. This may crush her but its weighing heavy on me.

It's now Saturday and we work only half a day on Saturdays and take off on Sundays unless we think we have spotted a good moving trick and flash our tray on him and he or she bites. Other than that, it's chillin on Sunday.

Today I will break the news to Venus about my change of mind to live in Houston and decided to let Mississippi be my place of residence. If she trips I'll deal with it because for real I'm missing Janice like crazy. Janice made me feel complete and appreciated. Venus really hadn't done anything else wrong – it was just the impact of what she had done and the way she had caused me to feel in the past few months. It has seriously changed my outlook concerning our relationship. No matter what I do or how hard I try to make this work I'm not feeling it nor am I happy. It's nothing Venus is doing at this time it's just the fact that the altercation has been done.

Some things you can't make right once a certain line has been crossed and the wedge that has been built between us seems to be one of those lines and it doesn't help that while this problem was rising between us, I had another shoulder to lean on.

L'il Tony has begun to try and talk and would say things such as "dada" and try to walk out the door every time I go towards that direction. One day he might be able to carry this torch and speak the language that will always allow him to eat and feed his family off the land. I never had a problem taking him with me because he was a good baby and not a problem with crying or always wanting you to pick him up. Plus the women always admired when you had a handsome little boy with you and wanted to cuddle him. This little joker had plenty of sense to be a toddler. If I could be blessed to give him this slum game he would never have to worry about being broke, fired or laid off anybody's job. All he would have to do is get up out of bed, not be lazy and find his man/woman somewhere in the four corners hiding in this great sweet country called America.

Antrice is trying to hold her own bottle but is also a daddy's girl. They're my reason, push and motivation that let's me know I have but one choice. That choice is to make sure they're alright and want for nothing, not even a kiss, smile, or a rub on the head to always assure them that daddy is here so they'll feel protected. They didn't ask to come into this world and now that they're here, it's our responsibility to keep it right for them and I'm welcoming the responsibility and challenge.

Chapter 19

Venus is not accepting going back to Mississippi too well - as I already knew she wouldn't. She's insisting that we continue on our journey to Texas. There's nothing she has said so far that sounds convincing enough for me to continue on in that direction. I'm not trying to hear it anyway and can't hear anything but Janice's voice in my mind pulling me back to Mississippi. The feeling is just too strong and has taken control over me and my mind is made up.

I finally got Venus to calm down and agreed to travel back to Mississippi and let the chips fall where they may. I guess she figured out she wasn't getting anywhere with me on the subject. Our relationship has, on the inside, totally deteriorated and all we're doing is pretending and going through the motions. We both know damn well at this moment it's over with no possibility of rectifying the situation.

One sunny afternoon between 12:30 pm and 1:00 pm, I'm in a comfort zone sleeping at Janice's apartment because I have made up my mind to completely let Venus go and stop going through the act of pretending or she was going to have to get with the program and follow. She's going to have to let me do my thing or get lost, one or the other.

While I'm sleeping Janice is sitting in the bed watching T.V. when all of sudden a loud thump is heard in the front living room. Not knowing at the time what was happening and whether or not somebody was trying to break in on us figuring I had some money in the house or on me because my reputation at the time of being a road hustler was known. I grabbed the .38 special I kept under the mattress. I never carried or traveled with a gun. A gun was not a necessity in my line of business and the game I was playing nor was it wise to carry one. I kept one around the house for my family's protection from the predators that will sometimes lay on what they might have thought was a sweet lick. I slowly got out of the bed and peaked around the corner of the bed room door. I put my finger to my lips in a gesture for Janice to keep quite. When I was able to get a better look I see a box in the middle of the living room floor as if somebody had thrown it through the door in a hurry.

Venus had thrown my clothes in the door of Janice's apartment to let me know not to come back and that she knew I was inside. By this time I didn't give a damn and wasn't thinking about coming back anyway. Truth be told I was happy she saved me the gas and hassle of coming to get them and having to deal with her foolishness. Before this event I hadn't talked to Venus in several weeks further burying what we once had and thought would last forever.

That part of the relationship is the true part that Venus refuses to tell our children the truth about. Venus would rather have them believe a lie and that we separated because of too many physical fights between us, which is not true. It happened at times but it wasn't the last straw that caused the separation and a fight had not happened in a while when I decided to move on. The bottom line was, I left Venus for Janice because I was tired of what we was going through and Venus trying to tell me what I should do when I'm making it work for us. I'm getting too much money at this time so there's no way I'm about to listen to her. Plus the incident of not coming to my rescue on the side of the highway had left a terrible taste in my mouth.

The fighting and arguing had ceased. I was not paying Venus any attention about anything if it wasn't concerning the children. I wasn't even touching her and cared less about what she did and didn't do. This is so, especially now that I'm deeply involved with Janice real strong. So the story that Venus has perpetuated over the years to Tony Jr. and Antrice is a lie that was told to them when they was at their most impressionable age. Since that time she has not been able to keep a man.

They're at the age now to where their understanding is much better and sight is clearer on matters. Sometimes you have to take a good look at yourself and the person in the mirror and stop blaming everybody else for your short comings.

I remember always telling my mama that so and so hit me first or so and so was bothering me or messing with me for the reason I did what I did and she would say, "There's no way every time something happens its always somebody bothering or messing with you Tony." Now that I look back, in hindsight, she was right. If you're always having problems then maybe you need to step back and check yourself.

Antonio Berry

Chapter 20

After going through the bull-shit with Venus for several weeks, around March-April 1984, Janice and I came together and started living as a couple. Venus, I had thought, would become a distant past even before the divorce. Things are going great between Janice and me, sex, money, traveling and we're spending quality time with one another and there's not enough time in a day for us. On many occasions Janice would travel from state to state with me and would, depending on the mood and the city, ride out to work with me some days to keep me company while I was on the prowl. It would be just the two of us sometimes on the road without my road partners. I had accepted her daughter Meeka, who was three years old at the time, as one of my own. She accepted me in her life just as happily and with grace.

We're now living in this apartment complex named Regency Woods Apartments in Pascagoula. Life couldn't be better I thought and if this is living to die then let me die. I'm driving the 77 Grand Prix I played the trick out of in Louisiana. This is now my on-the-road car and I'm doing my thing; me and Snap.

Another partner of mine named Rodney is also living in the complex with his family. Rodney was the slummer I mentioned earlier who was in Beaumont, Texas when we were run out of that city. Rodney was a very good slummer and we would ride out locally together whenever I was home for a short period of time. He also was a road hustler.

I had recently purchased, as my main automobile, a white on white '82 Regal Limited Edition with blue velour seats. Janice kept and drove this vehicle most of the time.

On this trip I decided to drive the Regal to work the city of Greenville, South Carolina. Snap followed me in a green Pontiac Catalina that he had recently paid $700.00 for in Mobile at a car lot on the corner of Broad Street. I was able to play the trick back for $300.00 of that same money for two watches and a chain in a jewelry box.

The first thing I did when we arrived in Greenville and checked into the motel is make a big fuck-up. My intention was to put up some of this good grade of weed for us to have something to smoke after we catch our trick and call it quits for the day. I'm moving too fast at the time and my mind was concentrating so much on trying to hide the weed that I placed it in the bathroom light fixture and left the light on. Or it could have been that one of us left it on in the middle of the night after going to use the bathroom. I really can't say but it was a big mistake. The light dried the weed to dust causing us to have to ride the local area in search of something to smoke. I never really minded this because it gave us the opportunity to find out who's who. This way when we were ready to leave the area we'll know who to spank for a sack of weed and cash.

A couple of weeks had passed and both snap and I have been sending a piece of the fruit of our labor home as always. I continue to send my Mom a portion of my earnings to put up for a rainy day and send Janice the remainder for our house-hold and the portion I wanted her to know about. I have never been down with letting people know where all my eggs were and I see no reason to begin now, not yet anyway.

I have no idea where Venus and my two children Tony Jr. and Antrice are living and it is her intent for me to not know. I've been informed by some of her family members that she's living in Houston. Venus thought this move by her would cause me to follow and chase behind her which she turned out to be very mistaken and it couldn't have been further from the truth. I'm in a comfort zone and satisfied with my current life, situation, and relationship with Janice, although I was having some sleepless nights worrying and wondering about my children's whereabouts and if they were alright or hungry because of some fool move made by their mother. Venus was trying to dictate my decisions and not knowing their whereabouts was eating at me like cancer.

I contacted Venus's mother who had always been sweet and treated me as if I was her son. She used to talk to me quite often trying to help solve the problems Venus and I was having. She used to always tell me I was a good man and commended me on how I took the responsibility to care for my children and her daughter but she didn't like the fighting. I once told her if I took care of everything in my house then I was going to run my house. I was young with a lack of life understanding that was necessary to see it any other way.

I spoke several times with Venus's mom and asked her to speak with Venus about figuring out a solution for me to contact her and the children. Or maybe get a P.O. Box so I could, at the very least, send some money to her for the children and not have them to suffer because of what we was going through as their parents. Venus finally took the initiative and made it possible through the means of a P.O. Box number and address.

Finally knowing their whereabouts and their condition stopped all the sleepless and stressful nights I was having. I had assured my conscience and was making it possible for them to have a roof over their heads and food on the table by sending something to their mother to help with their care as often as possible which was regular. It was many nights that I stressed in Janice arms missing them and having no idea of their current state of being.

Make no mistake about it, Venus would have died for them but she was doing something now that she hadn't experienced since they had been in this world and that was trying to survive with two children on her own with a workman pay. Our house-hold income had always been supplemented with what I brought to the table from the streets of America which was the majority. She was making a decision based on her emotions which was irrational.

Antonio Berry

Chapter 21

Snap and I had decided that Greenville, SC had given us all it was going to give and for no other reason except being satisfied as usual and wanting to get back to Janice, I packed up and we headed towards home after a couple of weeks of dragging that City. I put in the tape of the group "Utume" and listened to Juicy and You, Me, and He (what we're going to do baby) I listened to this all the way down 1-85 until it connected to 1-65 south onto I-10 west into Pascagoula, MS home of the Coast Playa's. I had no idea that if I had made it home several days earlier, I would have been the victim of a shooting and possibly dead by a deranged, crazy woman. This didn't set to well and caused me to put my guards up and be on alert for this crazy woman. I'm a firm believer that what's for you, you will get but this was something crazy coming at me from my children's mother. Venus had lost it and went off the deep end.

While living in Houston, Venus had continued to grow angrier, bitter and mostly jealous by the day because of the breakup and knowing I had moved on and was doing very good. She had begun to work at a McDonalds where she had become involved with some brother that was supposedly a manager or supervisor at the place. This was exactly the type of man she needed and wanted in her life, a square. I was too much of the streets for her, being I was out to not only break a trick's pocket but morals if they got in the way of this fire I was pushing and my way of eating. Which at the time it was the selling of these watches, chains, rings, bracelets and anything remotely associated with jewelry.

The brother Venus had gotten herself involved with had no idea she's crazy as a bug and that her heart is still misplaced. She takes this brother's automobile and I mean literally steals the man's car one day while he was either at work or lying in the bed after a day of good sex and drives the stolen car to Mississippi. He reported it stolen because he has no idea what the hell is going on and the fatal attraction similarity that he has gotten himself involved in with Venus. It's all coming out now and I guess it took an ordeal to occur to bring it to the light.

Venus made it to Mississippi in the stolen vehicle which is unbeknown to me because I'm still on the highway heading home from Greenville, SC at the time. Venus is riding around to all the popular hang-out spots with a gun in search of me and asking people had they seen me lately. She has gone over the cliff and is taking this breakup shit too far. The police pulled up on her with this Texas tag and run a check on the vehicle and discover the vehicle has been reported stolen. Venus is hauled off to jail for a stolen vehicle and possession of a firearm found in the vehicle. The police had no reason to suspect she was about to commit a murder.

Venus had come to Mississippi in a fit of jealous rage to commit a caper and flee back to Houston with me, a Coast Playa, as her victim. The local authorities probably would not have investigated the crime and rather just assumed someone I had coned out of their money had killed me and closed the case as a justified homicide. The woman had lost her marbles and wanted me dead. Her mind was made up that if she couldn't have me then she wasn't going to stand around and watch me with anybody else.

She could not live with the fact that I had moved on with my life and let her go with no concern whatsoever other than my children. You would think that if a woman has gotten herself another man and they were spending quality time together and he's taking care of his business, that she had no time to keep her ex-husband in her life, but that was not the case with Venus. I'm coming up in the world and happily in love with Janice while doing it and it's a wonder the fool didn't commit suicide based on her behavior. The charges were dropped and never heard of again and she went back to Houston to live, thanks to her brother Junior.

Chapter 22

Shortly after this episode and drama had settled down, I received a subpoena from the Youth Court Center that would change my life once again forever in a good way. An edition to my responsibilities was about to be added to my life, one that I welcomed whole heartedly. I always felt that being a man was also about taking care of your children so it wasn't a big deal, nor did I run from the responsibility. The subpoena was concerning what I heard from the streets but didn't know for sure at the time. It was that I had fathered another child by a different female that I had nothing but a sexual relationship with during a one-night stand maybe two or three times. Make no mistake about it the streets was screaming that I was the father but I hadn't seen the child and when ever I would see the mother Kristen, she would always say something totally different than what I was hearing and it was that I was not the father of her baby girl. Kristen was good people and fine as hell and pretty. She had actually wished all the talking would stop because she didn't want to cause any problems with her then-boyfriend who believed he was the father of this child. There was no way, if he heard the rumors, he could look at this child and not know.

I'm preparing for a child custody hearing that's a few days away and it has me full of anxiety. When I enter the door of the Youth Center and informed the reception of my name and reason for being there, she directs me down the hall to the room number where the hearing is being held. It turned out not to be what you would consider a hearing but a meeting. The first people I see when I entered the conference room was Kirsten, the mother, sitting to my right. The blamed father was sitting with his back to me and the door. The case worker was on the very far end of the table facing the opening of the door looking me straight in the eyes as if trying to make the comparison to the child concerning this hearing. She was a white lady with the expression on her face as if to say these are some disgusting young black people. I wasn't going to put up with her sarcasm because I felt like I was on top of the world and there wasn't anything she could tell me. Nor did I have to listen and if she went too far Janice was sitting at home with bail money and was only a call away. I'm hoping all the while that this white woman don't make me act a fool because of her view of me as a youngster not knowing I wasn't the average 19 year old black male.

I moved to the left farther in the direction of the case worker if that's what you could have considered her to be and had a seat.

"Good morning Mr. Berry," she stated. I knew damn well she didn't see me as a Mr.

"Good morning to you," I responded.

She proceeded to explain to everybody the nature of this meeting and allowed everybody to speak their opinion. She asked me did I need to take a blood test and would I be willing to sign papers admitting to being the baby's father for child support. I stated no to each and every question and explained my reason for said answer.

"The reason I say no is because I have two other children that's not with me due to a recent separation with their mother and a divorce that's in the process. I'm not and don't have to be forced to take care of my children. If they're mine that's all I need to know for me to do what I'm supposed to do as a father," I told her. I stated that Kirsten had been saying for her own personal reasons that her then-boyfriend was the baby's father and I'm not upset with her about that because obviously she was doing what she thought was best according to her situation at the time.

The blamed father looked down with great sadness in his eyes of a man that's defeated and saying, my God, this woman has mislead me for the last three years. Kristen really wasn't out there like that and I might have had only two or three more sexual encounters with her over the years after the baby was born. If she hadn't gotten pregnant for me they probably could have had an everlasting relationship without him ever knowing.

After stating my piece, I looked directly into Kirsten's eyes and asked her with all sincerity, because this wasn't a laughing matter, was the baby girl mine? Kirsten stated, "Yes."

Andraya, aka Tody, would be three years old in a couple of weeks. I said that I'm going to take care of her from here on and don't need to be forced to sign some agreement to do so because she's my child and that's all that matters to me.

The case worker then spoke up and said, "Mr. Berry if you're not going to sign the papers you may be excused and you will hear from the Court."

I never heard from the Court again and the reason was probably because I was a man of my word and Kirsten was good people. On the way out of the room I looked over at Kirsten and humbly said, "I'll be to get her and you know me well enough to know that if you're saying she's my child and I believe she is, you know you can believe I'll take care of her and don't need to be forced to do it." And I left the room with that said. Kirsten never placed me on child support. She and her mother have stated over the years that I did right by Tody.

Antonio Berry

Chapter 23

Tody was conceived from a one night stand, something that could be done in those days without taking the high risk of today's epidemics. My best friend at the time, Keith, now deceased, was dating one of my father's friend's nieces named Debbie. She and Kirsten were good friends and hanging out together regularly. I asked Keith to ask Debbie about hooking me up with Kirsten whom I thought at the time was fly, fine and very pretty and she really was. We all got together one day to hang out and ride around doing what we were doing in those days like turning a couple of corners smoking weed. We made plans for the next day to go swimming in the pool at my grandparents Mu-dear and Grand-daddy's' house in the pool they had built for the family in the 70's. These were my mother parents.

The next day after we had worked up a good appetite and work out from having fun in the pool, we took them home to where Debbie was living with her uncle and aunt who at the time was very good friends of my father. Keith and Debbie decided to venture into the house leaving Kirsten and I alone in my Dad's van that I happened to be driving this day. We're all in high school at the time and I think Debbie may have been the only one to have graduated. In the van that evening is where Tody's life begin. Kirsten and I never dated or became an Item in a serious relationship to be considered boyfriend and girlfriend. She was already in a relationship with a guy that had finish school ahead of us. He had left to join the army right after high school.

Once I returned home from the Youth Center, Janice was waiting on me to tell her how it had went. As soon as I came through the door she asked me how did it go? She had already been through the heart ache and pain with me in my situation of Venus and my children. Janice was concerned about my well being and state of mind and the effect this might have on me mentally because I had endured a heavy burden in the last year and was now going through some more babies mama drama. I proceed to give Janice a full detail play by play of what was said and asked and the responses given by me and the other individuals attending the meeting. Janice response was nothing less than what I had expected from her and her character. That is what separate a real true woman and the woman that thinks and act on her lower nature and lack the strength that's really necessary to stand strong by her man. The response Janice gave will forever be embedded in my mind, kind of like Jada Pickett acceptance of Will Smith and the package that came with him and his life. Janice simply said lets go get her.

From that day on Tody has known her father and she's a true blessing. Everybody think she looks and behave more similar to me than any of my other children.

My mother was a part time school patrol officer and had been seeing Tody with her grand-mother, Kirsten Mother when she was dropping one of her other grands off at West Elementary school most morning. My Mom had been hearing about this little girl I was suppose to have and I guess this particular morning something inside Mama made her tell Kirsten mother that she was the other grand-mother and wanted to keep her grand-baby sometimes. Tody had not yet reached the age to go to school.

Chapter 24

I came up with another scheme to supplement my income whenever I was home off the road. I hooked Janice sister up with a weed connection out of Houston, Texas and she begin to roll in the dough. When home from slumming on the road she would throw a couple of pounds my way for the same cost. This was appreciation for the hook up and plus I was her brother-n-law at the time. I'm 19 soon to be 20 and is surrounded by more money and events taking place than any 19 year old should be exposed to. Older people back then usually kept a youngster out of old folks business but my maturity and smoothness couldn't be denied so therefore I was exposed and privileged to more than the average youngster my age.

I knew damn near everybody and it wouldn't take me long to rid whatever amount of weed I had. It use to amaze Irma how I could just come straight off the road and take care of an altogether different type of business and hustle. I'm loving it and Janice but, the man-whore in me want let me be satisfied with just one woman or two for that matter. While at the house on a break from the road, most of the time I'll still be in bed when Janice leaves for work managing a convenient store by the name of Fayes Grocery. This would only be if I hadn't had my heart and mind set on a local surrounding state or City that I thought might be sweet and would pay a playa a little something extra while home. I usually try to save these local spots for the winter when all is needed is one or two days of work out of the week or for some reason when I was forced to be in town.

I will not mention names in this description of events that transpired during these hyped times in order to protect the innocent ones that almost went there but, didn't after a close call for whatever reason.

Also to protect the images and marriages of the ones that did go there which some has since changed their lives and moved on in a positive direction to make there marriages and lives turn out for the best. They were either victims or potential victims of my elaborate perfected trade mark scheme which was playing women like I played my tricks when slumming.

It was many mornings that it seemed like some female in the complex we were living might have been up all night waiting for Janice to leave for work the next morning. No soon as Janice would leave the apartment and she probably had not made it off the complex ground of the building, the door bell would ring. It had become a habit for them and myself because I would start to expect it to happen and actually looked forward to seeing who it was going to be this time. It would be one of several females that I either use to smoke or give weed to. They would show up at the door in their night gowns or wearing something less difficult to undress in.

During this era weed was very popular and people smoked it with a habit of not only loving it but having to have it. It wasn't as addictive as some of the drugs that came on the scene later. If Janice had once left something at the Apartment she needed to turn around for or got wind of what was happening and turned around, it's hard to imagine the sight of what possible might have happened. Because it was a regular occurring event and Janice would definitely fight.

Chapter 25

It was Janice, her daughter Meeka, who was three years old when we met and me. When the summer-time came around I would occasionally take them both on the road with me because like I said earlier, this game was less dangerous than known or think by some to be. By this time Janice had stop working. I was making more than enough to provide for three or four households. I use to hear all type of foolishness such as. Boy somebody is going to kill you about that fake jewelry. My response was always the same and that was. That's the exact reason I don't fuck with you broke negro's that can't afford to spend fifty cent but act like you have it. These Caucasians will take their lick as a lesson well learned or call the police to get their money back and sometimes us ran out of that City and then they're satisfied. A majority of white people is not about to send themselves to prison for buying some fake jewelry thinking they was getting a deal from somebody in the streets.

This was a way of life for me and one may believe that there was no principles in a man that could be doing such a thing but that couldn't be further from the truth. I've never conned a family member whether close or distant, friends, anybody that knew me because it was a line not to be crossed. Turk and some more of the fellows might mess with one another for simply humor but with no other intentions in the heart other than fun and a good laugh.

We might play on each other for a couple hundred and that was it. If you borrowed it you pay it back. Hell we have been taken by a good looking piece of slum when the brass pieces first hit the scene.

Janice would constantly remind me to watch what I say around Meeka especially using the word cracker because she was very impressionable at that age and she listened to every word you would say. I would sit around and be talking about how sweet a cracker was and how I played the trick that day calling them crackers this and crackers that because 98% of the times that's who it would be that paid me and allowed us to live in the comfort that we were living.

Meeka now is four years old and would blurt out in the malls, grocery stores or wherever she may be when she sees a white person and it comes into her little mind, she would scream out and call a white person a cracker. To keep them from sitting around the motel room bored all day when they was on the road with me, I would come in at 12:00pm if I wasn't satisfied and close by and take them back out with me to work the second half of the day. One day while working the Tampa, Florida area and only having grinded up a couple of hundred a day I decided to swing back by the Golden Penny Inn off 1-4 to take Janice and Meeka to lunch-and see if they wanted to ride to work with me that second half. The way I was playing the slum game it was safe for them to ride with me.

Blacks wanted to and would kill you over fifty cents while most white people will take their loss and pass it on. Don't get it misconstrued because they to would sometimes scream foul play but not as often as the blacks if you tricked one of them which is the reason I stayed away from them. Brothers or anybody for that matter who I would tell about the game and how I was playing it across the Country will say that they would have killed me, even when I didn't strong armed them and they gave me their money willingly. The white man been lying to you all your life and you haven't killed a bunch of them nor complained about the over-priced products he's been selling you while under paying your dumb ass. But that's the black man for you, always doubt and undermining the next black man. All I would and could tell them was to stay out of the line of fire and they wouldn't get burned.

Janice, Meeka and I are riding in Tampa with me pulling in and out of different businesses with me trying to find a trick that would immediately send us back to the room or to another City altogether. If I conclude they're not biting or one bit too hard I will not take the chance of giving the lick back and just move on. I'll sometimes have Janice to pull the car further up or her and Meeka can go inside one of the McDonalds or whatever other eating place is around and sit and wait for me to come up the street. I'll work my way to them and she would have the car park so I can see it while moving in that direction.

I pulled up in front of this business and starts to prepare to go inside with the arranging of my jewelry in the jewelry tray with the price tag before going in and presenting my goods to the boss or whoever decides to get in the way of this bullet I'm packing. I'll rather see the boss because he's the one who signs the checks. I also make these arranging to assure there is no bad piece of jewelry that might cause the trick to be suspicious once I get them on line. I opened my door and feel the back of my seat being pushed up from the rear as if somebody is attempting to get out from the back seat faster than I am. I looked back and it's Meeka with a shocker. I said where do you think you're going and what are you trying to do?? It was unbelievable, the shocking words that came from her mouth left both, Janice and me gasping for air and tie tongued. Meeka said she's trying to go in there and sell that cracker some gold. From that day on, I would never do or say anything in the presence of my children that could have a bad influence or embarrassment to Janice or cause one to question their home training.

The last day of working Tampa came about because of some heat I got from the local authorities as well as a threat. I guess they had gotten some calls but nobody that asked for their money to be returned. I can see the police cars riding up and down the strip but I really don't know exactly why. Slummers have a hunch about this sort of things when they see the cops riding and scouting. Usually someone has called them and they're trying to locate or recognize us if they don't have a description of the car. Most of the time its only reported that we're walking up and down the street trying to sell some jewelry.

They finally spot me and pull me over and asked for some ID. I'm not trying to hide and more trying to let them do what they do and move on about their business so I can get back to my work. I give them my ID and answer all of their side-way smart ass questions. They look at the jewelry real good, throw a lot of remarks out in the air and politely say that if I don't leave Tampa with this fake shit that's stamped 14kt, that they have a building down town on Morgan Street with people that deals in this type of crime and said if I didn't believe them to just try it by not leaving the area. America is too big for me to force myself on Tampa, Florida. So I just as politely say in my Country slang, thank you sir and you'll have a nice day and you want have to worry about me in Tampa ever again, I'm gone. Submission is all they're seeking on most occasions and that's what they got from this Coast Playa.

Photo Album

Military photo of author Antonio Berry, age 17

Author Antonio Berry with his brothers & sister

Antonio's Aunt Vera and Uncle Billy

Grand Daddy & cousin Tosha Dubose

Grand Daddy Johnny   My Dad's Father

Antonio Berry

Grandfather Lawrence

Grandmother Mu-Dear

Janice, Meeka & Tara's mother

January 2012
Daddy Johnny, Tara, the Author, Tody
grandchildren

Jeff & Tina-Bit

Kristen Lewis
Aka
Tody's mom

The author and Bettie

The author and Red Charles
At Dunn River Falls in
Ochorios Jamaca

Me, Antrice & grandchildren

**The author, Janice, Red Charles, Arlene, & Claude
In
Cancun Mexico**

The author, Lil' Tony & AJ, III

Xmas, 2011
The author, Antonio Berry
At
Yazoo City Federal Penitentiary

The author as a child with Darryl & Eric

1992 Easter Sunday
At church in the 64 Chevy
The author with Meeka & Tara

Meeka & Tara
sitting on my Kamari kitted Maxima in Orlando

The author's children
Tody, Meeka, Lil'Tony
Tara, Antrice

My dad's Mother
Grandma Big Momma

The author's green 300 AMG Benz

The author's mother, Shirley

The author's sister, Sharon
Standing beside the author's 78 Seville

Road partner, Snap & his grandson

**The author's sister,
Sharon & Grand Daddy Lawrence**

The author sitting in his 190 E Benz

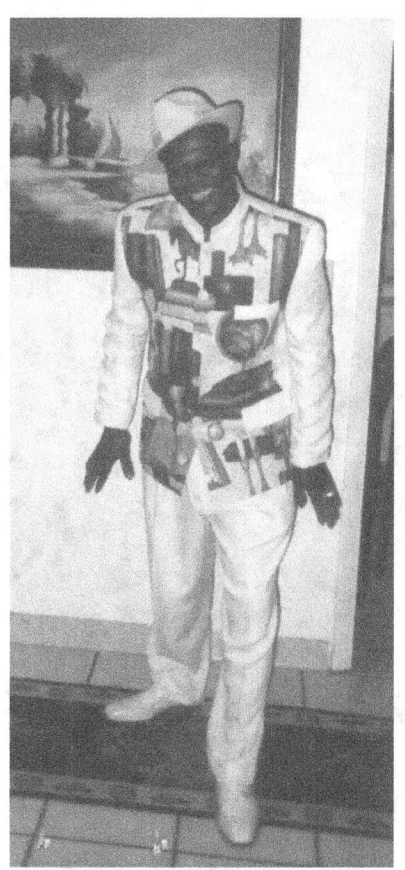

Turk, master of the game

Venus
Lil'Tony & Antrice's mom

Chapter 26

It's still 1985 and a lot has happened this year but nothing has changed in the way we're riding and getting paid except in the way we have experienced some tricks responses to the game. I had continued to carry Darryl with me after he graduated from High School in an attempt to give him this game that's invaluable. That was this game as it's played by only a few and executed to perfection by even fewer.

There would be times when a trick has either been burned or knew we were trying to burn him or they truly thought we had stolen the jewelry. They would be good citizens and call the police or respond in a manner that could have gotten somebody killed. It was jail or hell in the minds of some of these tricks for us who they thought was scums and no good ass Negros who might have ripped off some of their people. Most would just say no and let you move on without another thought about you coming into their place of business. They wouldn't care one way or the other and just didn't want any part of what you had to offer or sell even if you was giving it away.

Nothing stay on my mind more than the time I had Darryl riding with me one day over to work Bay Minette, Alabama in Baldwin County. Darryl had the good fortune of catching tricks the way I would when I first started in the game that eventually lead up to Turk telling me I had to work out of my own car. This did not start for me until Turk realized I was able to drain my tricks for all they had and he couldn't go in behind me and get one dime. Darryl has yet to perfect the skill of draining a trick he catches so I was always able to let him ride with me because he was very lucky when it came to going into a good spot. Once he catches them I would go in behind him and make them spend more than they had originally said they had. The object was to make one trick pay the both of us for that day.

Darryl had been in this one place of business in Bay Minette too long and my mind is racing and want let me sit still any longer without thinking that the trick may be holding him up without Darryl being able to detect whether or not the trick is biting or playing games to siphon information. Tricks do this to determine if what they're thinking is true, if the jewelry is stolen so they could call the police. This place is a cabinet business and it's sitting behind a bank. Darryl has been in there for more than fifteen minutes and that's more than enough time to determine whether or not the trick is going to spend any money.

When I stepped in I see the jewelry laid out on the boss desk top and Darryl is talking to him about what I had assumed to be the amount he was asking for the entire tray. I walked up and Asked what was happening and what was Boss talking about doing. Darryl stated that boss said he'll give him $300.00 for the tray which consisted of two Omega's replica watches and two gold plated chains, a total value of $28.00. Now here I am a seasoned veteran who can think about nothing else but this being a good trick and trying to take him to the bank up front.

I eased into the conversation with the famous cap line and tell Boss to look here, you might as well get everything we have so we can get the hell from over here without seeing or asking anybody else in this town and we can leave as quietly as we came with nobody being the wiser. Boss said let me see what else you have son. After carefully looking over the jewelry I had laid out for him, I started to get a bad feeling and asked boss was he the police with all the questions and hesitation and he said no he wasn't the police. Boss then said all he had was a check. I tell him that's cool because I have my ID and all he has to do is call the bank and let them know I'm coming so they want think I stole your check book. He had me thinking he was going to give us $2,600.00.

Boss reached in for what I thought was his check book and came up with what looked like a 1845 colt revolver from the civil war era. Boss started screaming for us to get up against the wall you thieving ass nigga's and put your hands up high before I blow your got damn brains out. This cracker is shaking with his finger on the trigger. He has taken his mind all the way off Darryl because he's thinking now that I'm the ring leader of this crew of thieves with Darryl appearing to be young and to top it off I came in and took over the conversation and show this cracker something that was two good to be true. A nigga with sense but the threat was a nigga with nerves to come in his place of business with this shit. All I can do now is try to talk this fool with this pistol down and in a state of calmness and hope this gun don't go off before he settle down long enough to hear me out. I'm trying to tell him that the jewelry is not stolen and nothing but cosmetic jewelry and that we're peddlers with a license to sell from business to business and the license is in my back pocket. The cracker is not trying to hear nothing I am saying and without even looking at Darryl he tells me to lay face down on the floor and shut up. Darryl is pleading with me to be quiet and do what he say. I remarked with venom that somebody needs to talk to this man. He finally say he's going to call the police and that's the best sound and words I've heard in the last two or three minutes which lead to me saying please call them.

The police arrived and begin to try and get some understanding of what was going on because I had check with the dispatcher who knew I was out there roaming about so this had the police confused. One cop ordered me to get up off the floor. While getting to my feet and being escorted out the door of the business to separate us, I stated that somebody needs to talk to that fool because he's going to hurt an innocence person.

They talked to him for a few minutes and came back out and tell Darryl and I where a car load of cops was watching us, to leave that City and never come back with that bull-shit again. I said fuck them on the way out and just had to ask the last joint on the outskirts of town before we hit I-10 West in an attempt to get paid for all the humiliation I had been subjected to. Most of all it was the arrogant and adrenaline on my part to play the game like a Coast Playa.

Chapter 27

There was another instance when we where working Sarasota, Florida and Darryl goes into this boat repair joint. The building was long in the front and you had to walk a hundred yards to reach the counter. Darryl went in to holla at the Boss and had been in for what I thought was long enough to have Boss going over the edge or what was necessary to make a factual determination as to whether or not Boss was a potential trick. I contemplated a few more minutes before making my mind up to go in and see if he had the trick down and was working the mark.

I'm thinking based on the size of the building and company that this might be a good lick. I reached the counter and politely asked the lady standing on the opposite side had she seen the guy come in looking for the Boss with some jewelry and her hands immediately went up to cover the opening of her mouth and said at the same time that, if you're with him, my Boss just ran him out the back. I retreated the same way I came in but with caution. I proceeded to the car and backed out of the parking lot and headed down the side street where I thought Darryl might be coming which was the only way he could come from this dead end street, and what did I see??? Darryl running for his life trying to get away from the dogs Boss had sicced on him once he cleared the threshold of the entrance point. The tricks sometimes had a tendency to sic their dogs on you for whatever the reason could have been. It could have been that they had been swindled before, knew that you were trying to swindle them, prejudice or just thought you was another nigga trying to sell some stolen goods. I had to one time jump through the sun roof of my car once because once I turned around to walk away the boss had sicced his dog on me.

Chapter 28

While working Fort Pierce, Florida on a rainy day trying to find my man in this bad weather, I entered inside a car lot business after splashing through some water and cursing like hell from getting wet hoping this is the one. Its two guys sitting in a office with no door attached. One looked like a drug dealer the other was a pot belly looking Buddha sitting there as if he's one hamburger from a stroke. Pot belly turned out to be the boss of the place. I flashed the tray on them both and the one that looked like the drug dealer with all the jewelry on grab at the tray and took it out of my hand. First thing came to mind Oh shit I'm about to be jacked. To my surprise he began to examine the contents as if he was interested. I'm nervous now because this one appears to be strong in whatever game he was in and I know if he paid me, I must leave this area.

He continued to examine the jewelry in the tray for a couple more minutes then asked what did I want for it?? Not knowing and can't get a feel for whether this was a set up or not I played myself by asking for fifteen and left it at that. Boss asked me to come back in an hour. My mind is now running a hundred miles an hour trying to figure out whether to come back or not. I decided to go by the room and tell Janice to lets pack because if he pay me we're leaving. I been here for a week anyway and the City is not that big.

When I pulled back up to the car lot I was being cautious of my surrounding, I see boss waiving for me to come in and the first thing I think is, Shit I hope this is straight. It may be a trap but I'll let it play itself out. Pot Belly is still sitting there and it looks like they had just completed lunch which now I'm thinking is the reason they asked me to come back. I must have caught them in the middle of having lunch.

The rich looking one that appears to be a drug dealer with all the jewelry on ask could I follow him home. I want say where this house was but I did. When we pulled up the first thing Janice said was, Tony I don't know about this. The look of this mansion in Indian River County scared the hell out of Janice because it looked like a member of a Mob home for real. I told her to just sit in the car while I go in. I had a heart of steal especially when it came to chasing money. The front entrance was set up with glass mirrors and the way the mirrors was placed you could see from deep back in the den area to the front door. You could see the person from the time they entered the front door until they made their way to the den. The upstairs stairway went up in a spiral of glass mirrors all the way to the second floor.

It's too late to turn back now and I feel more relax because anybody would not invite you to their home with intention to do harm and he looked like he could have a lot to lose. Boss tells me to come on back. It's nobody but him and me and he takes another look at everything as to make sure it's the items he'd seen earlier and asked me again what's the least I'll take.

I quickly responded, "Boss fifteen is giving it away."

He countered with, "I'll give you eleven and when you get some more come see me."

With this the only thing I can say is, "Boss for real, because I don't want to be getting this shit on a promise thinking you're going to take it off my hands and then you renege on me after I've sold you these pieces real cheap."

I took the eleven hundred and left the house in one direction toward St Lucie County on A1A South and rode for about a mile or two and turned around and went the other way; north toward Brevard County to throw off the direction I left if he was watching. I'm leaving this area for good like the Coast Playa I am.

Chapter 29

Snap and I also worked West Palm Beach, Stuart, Bell Glades and other cities from Boca Raton and up the Florida East Coast. We would always, when in the area, dock and get a room at the Days Inn or the Knights Inn that sits behind the Days Inn off 1-95 and 45th Street exit.

The very first time we docked there and decided to work I went to jail after spending several hours going through the red tape trying to secure a county license. My intent was to use them to work the entire county, including the cities, pretending not to know that I needed one for each individual city.

Boca Raton is the first city we're going to work with the plan being to work the county end to end from bottom to top. Someone had called the local police as soon as we begin to work the businesses, notifying them that we were out and about. We hadn't bothered to check in with them because we were trying to circumvent a procedure. Also this was Florida, a high traffic density area. We figured the local police receive a lot of calls concerning peddlers and we wouldn't be something new for them to see.

When the cops arrived on the scene to check out what the call was about they asked for our drivers licenses and we presented them along with our county peddler's license that we had applied for not even an hour earlier. We had made sure to ice all the places we entered because we knew what we was doing was border-line illegal concerning working a city area with nothing but a county license. The cops insisted on running us through their crime check computer and said if we cleared we could be on our way and good luck. They had no idea of the game we was playing and actually wasn't even interested in the jewelry.

My brother Darryl is with us at this time and we're standing on the side of the road while people are passing by and slowing down. Probably wondering what is going on with the three young black guys that the police have on the side of the road. I can imagine what might be going through some of their minds. They probably are thinking that we must have tried to rob someone, carjacking or plane racial profiling because of the area. Neither is the correct assumption. We're trying to rob but not the type of robbery that could be on their minds.

Ten minutes later two more car loads of police pull up and now there are about five policemen and us. This scene don't look right and just as I was saying and thinking this, one of them asked me to step over to his car and turn around. He explained that I had a warrant out on me for failure to appear in Defuniak Springs, Florida and Pinella County, Florida. I tried to explain to them that I was told on both occasions that if I didn't appear, the bond money I posted would go toward the fine and the matter would be resolved. They weren't trying to hear none of it. They had gotten a call and were able not to let it be a blank mission call, somebody was going to jail and it was me.

The fact was that every time I was stopped and arrested I posted a cash bond and was sometimes told that if I didn't show up for court, the cash bond would go toward the fine and I would be cleared. That's not what appears to have happened in this case. I never went back to court in those places where I was told that because it wasn't worth it if I was on the other side of the country. Bond was always $300.00 to $400.00 for mostly suspended drivers licenses or reckless driving and somebody was going to give me that much in one day. It didn't make sense to waste an entire week for one day of pay. Especially if I was in Oklahoma or North Carolina to come all the way back to Florida for court just to end up giving them the money anyway. So that's what I had intended to do on these two occasions on these two warrants. I was hoping they would keep the money and clear my name.

In 1985 the county jail in Palm Beach County was new. It was on Gun Club Road and had not yet been completed and I guess they were trying to get every dime they could from traffic stops and fines. I stayed in jail there for two or three days until my Mom could get it cleared up. My Mom went to the Moss Point, Mississippi Police Department and had them to do some tele-typing to help straighten this problem out. She was a school patrol lady for the department at the time. Defuniak Spring and Pinellas County had to check their records to verify what I was saying about I was told what would happen if I forfeit the bond I paid. Then both of them tele-typed Palm Beach and I was cleared and released. Now somebody was going to pay this Coast Playa.

Chapter 30

We did some dipping in the dope game back then but it wasn't anything serious just something to make each trip pay for itself since we were coming up out of Florida. During these days Florida was cocaine capital.

After working Palm Beach on one of the trips and having come up with a decent bank roll, we decided to try Miami. Miami city was very hard to catch tricks in. They weren't buying jewelry off the street because everybody was wearing the flea market jewelry and jewelry was always being exchanged for dope and there was plenty of that around. We worked the Miami area for about two weeks and after being on the road for a month, all Snap and I had was around $1,500 to $2,000 each and we was ready to take it in. With motel fare, drinking and the smoking, this city was eating at our bank roll.

I had been kicking it with my cousin Tez whom is now deceased. I often think about him because we had always been close. We had once lived in Miami in the sixties and it was a time when my grand-father dropped me and my cousin Myron off in Miami for the summer. Myron was Tez's brother who was raised by Mu-dear and grand-daddy. We would spend the entire summer in Miami and later when I was older I use to travel down there myself to visit. So Tez and I had always been close.

Whenever snap and I finished up for the day we would go by and scoop Tez. He introduced me to some brothers that was living in Cherry Bay that was doing their thing and having plenty money at the time. Contrary to belief and what the family and friends may still believe, Tez was not into anything illegal and I'll stand on that because I was doing the streets and he could have been but wasn't. His death was really something to where he was in the wrong place at the wrong time.

He had just gone to Atlanta behind his Mom, Dad and the rest of his family moving that way. He just happened to be sitting in a car that belong to somebody else that was having beef with another group of guys that Tez had no knowledge of. So get over the myth of belief that he was doing something illegal.

The guys in Cherry Bay were getting real dope money throwing bricks at the rock but that's what was happening in that time and place. It was not something Snap and I was interested in for a career purpose but we felt we had something sweet. We could score a little dope to take back to Mississippi and get rid of it before anybody realized it was us that had it.

It had been slow these last couple of days in Miami - actually the entire two weeks while we were there. But we kept grinding, barely coming up with rent money. We still had the habit of smoking weed and the occasionally drinking of a beer or sipping of cognac on the weekend.

This life style brings a lot of the finer things in life that the average working man can't do and will never be able to do but also this type of life style can bring destruction to the mind, body and soul and it's expensive. So in the end it can sometimes be nothing to glamorize.

The new friends we have met from Cherry Bay know that we're from out-of-state and tell us what we can get and for what prices. In a way this sounds foreign to us because we haven't been keeping up with the prices of ounces and kilograms of cocaine. Weed was something different because it was something we had the occasion to buy from time to time.

Thoughts are going through our minds about how much we can earn. If we pay $500.00 for an ounce and can make anywhere from $2,500 to $3,000 in Mississippi then we might need to think real serious about scoring a couple of ounces. It's not something we're trying to get into but since we're heading to the house what would be the harm.

Snap and I put our money together and scored a couple of ounces and at this time we had no idea how dangerous and detrimental this drug could be if we were caught in possession of it. We stashed it under the dash board and rode up Hwy 27 North until we got to Tampa and hit 1-75 trying to see I-10. There was a feeling about being out of the danger zone once you hit I-10.

We make it home safe and sold the package with no problem and the profit was good and the smokers wanted more of this from-the-bottom-of-Florida product. It was raw and straight from the bottom in Miami the way it came from South America. This was not going to be a continuing practice for Snap and me; at least that's not what our plans are. As a matter of fact Miami had left a bad taste in our mouth as far as the slum game was concerned and we had no intentions of heading back that far down in South Florida anytime soon. It had been our plan not to return.

1985 had been the best year for us because Snap and I was able to bounce from state to state, city to city and was having more money than we had ever had. North and South Carolina at the time looked like pretty good picking from the map with many small cities with the population ranging in the 25,000 to 50,000 people. The bigger the city, the easier it was to hide on the other side of town after work. You could work big cities until you just about burned the entire area completely up with nobody else to ask.

When we docked in an area we would always work the largest city last and drag it from strip to strip. Ashville, Chapel Hill, Durham, Raleigh, Fayetteville (The Merc), Greenville, High Point and many more cities in North Carolina felt our wrath. Oh I can't forget about Charlotte, you owe me nothing.

I'm not exaggerating when I say we were some of the coldest flat foot road hustlers at this time that America was encountering. The cold war and Reagan-nomics era had people's minds elsewhere and fraud wasn't a focus of concentration in most District Attorney's offices.

Fayetteville, North Carolina was our first stop and the most memorable city. It was not only because of the way the tricks were biting and paying us but also because of a certain individual we met during our stay and venture in this city. We were living at the Holiday Inn on 1-195 loop truck route. This Holiday Inn, at that time, was a one level flat building with a Waffle House across and down the street a few yards away to the left. We had made this our place to grab breakfast on the way to work every morning.

Fayetteville was sweet and you have to keep in mind the Army base that's located there and the way we're playing this game and the way we're bringing it from town to town with no mercy. This was all new to this area of businesses, even the ones that thought they had seen and done it all, they hadn't seen this. They too were potential victims of this slum game; nobody was immune if they got in the way. You could visit that city today and it would probably be just as sweet if not sweeter than it was then. This is so, not only because of the constant changing of military personnel, but also because of citizens moving and children operating businesses that were once owned and operated by their parents. If you couple this with the fact that a sucker is born every minute and second of the day you could definitely find you a trick in Fayetteville.

There's a strip in the hood that the locals call "The Merc" and its where Snap and I would visit everyday after work to score us a sack of weed. It's booming in this area, people are everywhere hanging out like it's a festival. A neighbor-hood Laundromat seems to be the main loitering place. You could either take a right and head in the direction of The Merc or turn left and head in the direction of Fort Bragg. This was how close the base was to the hood and the possible reason for so much money being in this area. Fayetteville was a fast moving semi-small City and you had to be on your square because of all the sort of games that was being played and executed, from acting to white-slavery.

Anyone of the characters played could get you bagged or placed in hand-cuffs. Pimping seems to be one of the oldest, famous, infatuated and admired games and was played everywhere. It was completely noticeable and being executed all over America as if it was legal during these times. You would look at such behavior and savor the moment and idea that you're part of this play in the under-world that's playing a major role in the developing of society.

Chapter 31

One night while Snap and I was lying around the room in Fayetteville smoking weed and watching the local news. This was something we always did just in case the city was screaming our identity and game on the local air news and informing the public to be aware of the bandits and the most recent con game that was being played on their local citizens and business owners.

A news flash came across the television screen announcing that a suspect in a large prostitution ring had been arrested for white-slavery along with more than twenty prostitutes he had prostituting the Fort Braggs area. Another suspect, the recent arrestee's partner was considered the ring leader of this organization and master-mind of this plot that included more than fifty prostitutes, was still being sought by the police at the time of this broadcast. His aka street name is Green-eyes and they asked that if anybody knows his whereabouts to contact the Fayetteville police department.

I told Snap, "Damn, those Negro's are pimping for real."

We knew the sight of true pimps because of some hellu-va pimps from around our way at the house. One in particular, a pimp legend named Jimmy and a few others that was getting trap money. It showed by the women, homes, automobiles, clothes, jewelry and just the style of life he was living. I won't mention the others and only mention Jimmy's name because I know him personally and I know in my heart he's alright with me mentioning his name because he understands and knows the playa that's telling this story to be a real Coast Playa of the under-world game.

The next morning we start the day with our regular routine of waking up and preparing ourselves to do what we do. Before leaving or beginning to ask anybody in search of a trick, we stop by the front desk to pay today's rent for that day and then stop by the Waffle House for breakfast. You always pay your rent before pulling out in the morning if you're going to stay another night so that the room will be attended to. We're serious about our business. When you're hundreds of miles from home and this is your way of surviving on the road and getting bills at home paid, you can't play with it physically or mentally. You have to have that get up and go about yourself. We always called it flat-foot hustling.

As we pulled in the parking lot of the waffle house, I notice a slant back Seville Cadillac that I'm not really paying that much attention to at first. I can't really remember what color it was but when it finally dawned on me and I noticed it, it was only because it could have been my first potential trick of the day. It's early and I'm not all the way awake yet.

I grabbed my tray of jewelry and began to arrange the pieces in the tray, so you already know what's on my mind.

We eased in and found us a booth and placed our order with the waitress while looking around scouting the joint trying to see who could be driving that Seville sitting out-side. There was three people sitting directly behind Snap and facing me. Two black men and one chocolate-skinned black woman. I immediately noticed one of the guys with what I thought was some funny looking eyes until I paid more attention and seen that they were green. In this day and time color contact lens was not popular.

I haven't paid any more attention to the Seville Cadillac outside. I'm now observing the surrounding people in the restaurant when I come to the conclusion that it must be these three individuals that own the Seville. They look as if they've had a long night or drive.

As I'm thinking of an approach, I take another look at the Seville and notice something I didn't see at first - it had a tag in the front with a green eye painted in the center.

I then tell Snap to take a look because that's the guy or guys that was on the news about the pimping charge. He thinks I'm tripping until he turns around and sees for himself and draws the same conclusion.

We're debating whether to crack the tray open on them inside the restaurant or let it pass for now. Our old phrase came to mind. We had a saying; a closed mouth can't get feed.

The broad noticed me watching and I guess she's thinking I'm a trick and may want to buy some sex, not knowing my behavior is an attempt to get their attention so I can flash this tray of jewelry on them. I'm trying to do it with as much discretion as possible and not be obvious to the other patrons, employees and manager of the establishment. I didn't want to offend them by soliciting inside their domain without permission. I finally flashed the tray on them and the guy with the green eyes gives me the wave that he passes and was not interested as if he has a million other things on his mind and spending money on a street deal was not one of them at this moment. The guy really appears to have some serious shit on his mind and didn't want to be bothered.

I was determined and wasn't about to give up on what I thought was a sweet potential trick and one that could be vulnerable due to heavy shit on their minds. I can't remember how the conversation got started between them and Snap and I but one did. I explained to them that we had seen the local news. Green-eyes knew the game we were playing and confirmed that was him on the local news broadcast.

We discussed the game that each was playing in these streets and chopped it up for a few minutes. This pimp was clocking dope money in the ho game. What amazed Green-eyes at the time were my age and spunk and the ability and the willingness and courage to actually take this underworld street game and run with it across the country at such a young age. Playa's such as himself know that whoever taught this young brother the game has to be a master because it shows in the student. Every now and then the student's skills excel beyond that of his teacher but that comes with time and practice. I was too young to have much time and practice under my belt but I was fast becoming a top notch Coast Playa.

Chapter 32

At one point we had decided that we all, Turk, Jeff, Rodney, Chuck, Mickey, Chico, Snap and I, would venture together and tour the Carolina's and work our way to Virginia. Before we could get a good days work in Carolina around the Raleigh-Durham area, the state Troopers and local authorities escorted us to the interstate and politely asked us to leave their area with the bull-shit. As always, we did what they asked so we could live another day to catch our man, sleeping somewhere else in another state and city.

There were about five car loads of us on this trip looking for a spot to terrorize. I was driving the '77 Grand Prix I had played the trick out of in New Orleans, Turk was in his yellow/brown Mercedes, Jeff was in a '64 white and red Galaxy, Chuck was in a beige duce and a quarter and Chico was in a black Cutlass. We're rolling the hills of Virginia when Jeff's car starts giving him problems. Now he has to make a tactical decision about what to do; put the car in the shop or leave it. Somebody got lucky and came up good because we left it. Turk remembered a white boy that had never seen a black man before anywhere in those mountains. I can't honestly say I remember the white boy.

We finally make our way to Norfolk, Virginia and docked on Military Circle and Beach Blvd. across from the mall. The Bennigan's in the mall was my favorite eating place for the baby-back ribs and you could get a glass of liquor with your meal.

Norfolk wasn't a bad place and actually had that down-south feel that we were use to. We would ride across the bridge to the neighborhood in the vicinity of Norfolk University. In this same 'hood a couple blocks down and make a left turn, you could find a strip and hang-out area with the hustlers and cop a bag of weed or whatever. There were so many broads around this campus it was pathetic. Then after working up an appetite we would ride to Portsmouth to Poor Folks for the red beans and rice.

Two car loads of us decided one morning to ride south to the same place and work that area together. We rode south on Beach Blvd. to a city named Chesapeake. There were five of us all together between the two cars that were heading that way. We're going up and down the strip until we run into the car that Rodney and somebody else is working in. Rodney had caught what we believed might be a good trick to pay everybody; a man we took it on our own to call Mr. Bob. He was alright with us calling him that not knowing we're calling him that with the concept of being a John/trick. He didn't want us knowing his government name anyway being he thinks he has gotten the deal of the century.

Rodney told us that Mr. Bob was about to give him $600.00 or $700.00 and hopped in the large Tonka truck with Mr. Bob and told us to follow them. We followed Mr. Bob and Rodney to a bank where Mr. Bob withdrew the first large sum of money.

When Rodney finished with him and got all he thought he could get he let the other piranha's chew on him. We got the remainder he had and was willing to give up to us. When we let Mr. Bob go and he had pulled off and got free from the grip we had on him, Mr. Bob had released about $3,000 to $3,500 between the five of us. He was our first trick upon the arrival and first day of work in Norfolk.

We're still in Norfolk when Snap, Jeff and I pull up into this florist shop and presented the tray of jewelry to a middle aged, sexy looking white woman who turned out to be the owner. I was the first to get paid from her which wasn't but about $300.00 to $400.00 for a few pieces which you can always believe was a win for me. We worked her the same way as we did all tricks that bit and there was more than one of us in the car. We always try to make one pay all. The same as with Mr. Bob, everybody got a piece of the trick.

After getting what I was going to get I made my way back to the car and crawled into the back seat ducking like it would prevent me from giving back the fruit I had just come up with. Snap was driving because it was his day to do so. Nobody really cared to drive because it broke your rhythm trying to keep up with the car and everybody. You might get a check and if the bank was on the other side of town you needed to get there before the trick wakes up and cancels the check. I've had that happen by not getting to the bank fast enough. It had been a time when I didn't know where the car was parked and headed out walking to the bank and by the time I get there the trick had called the bank and told them to tell me to come back and see them. I didn't know if it was to spend some more money or didn't want the jewelry or had called the police, so I had to take that loss and let them have it because it could have been a set up.

I'm lying low hoping Jeff and Snap would hurry up with the lady in the florist so we could leave this spot and get a six-pack and fire up a joint of weed. Then we could head back toward the room in Norfolk or towards the campus to flirt with some broads. There was a ladies ring in my tray that the Boss Lady had eyes on and wanted but I played hard with her and wouldn't give it up unless she coughed up what I had asked for it. It didn't make sense to give it up if I could play without having to. I ended up taking the piece back to the car with me and let Jeff and Snap pound on her for a while. Tricks will always tell you they have no more money but will come up with some for a different face if his cap game might be stronger that day.

Everybody had got what they were going to get from her and made it back to the car. Jeff was real slick and knowing the woman wanted the ring I had, Jeff blew some dust my way in the air. This dust caused me to push the seat up from the back trying to get back in this florist as fast as possible. One thing about this type of selling I'm thinking about to take place is, you don't have to worry about the trick screaming because it would be too embarrassing.

What Jeff said was that the Boss Lady wanted to work something out like a deal for the ring. He made it sound like she meant sex in exchange. Hell I'm twenty years old, this middle age, sexy looking, and possibly rich, white lady wanted to give me some sex for a $2.50 ring after giving me a few hundred for $30.00 worth of slum. I'd be a damn fool not to run in and check this out.

I jumped out of the car and run back in there and called the Boss Lady back to the front counter and spit the conversation cap on what I think is the truth from Jeff. Boss Lady is looking confused as if what the hell am I talking about and all I can say is that my buddy said you wanted to see me again about the ring and maybe we could work something out. By this time her son has came from the back of the shop and asked is everything ok? I say yes and was just showing your Mom this ring again that my buddy said she wanted to see while at the same time playing my way for the door to exit this scene.

When I make it back to the car I cursed Jeff's ass out for that foul shit he just pulled and told them both we almost had to give all the money back because the woman was appearing to be offended. They started laughing as if it was funny and telling me to stop tripping and being fast Freddy. That's where I got the second street name of Freddy; from Jeff and his games.

We laid there in Norfolk for about two more weeks before moving on to another side of the country to introduce these Coast Playa.

Chapter 33

Sweet Little Rock, Arkansas was definitely in the top five sweetest states and cities we ever worked. Tricks there were paying $200.00 to $600.00 for one dollar Cz's. Every week was a $4,000 or better week for the both of us. We had struck a gold mine and it was unbelievable that it seemed as if nobody there had ever seen the game or doubted the goods we were pushing. Hot Springs, Arkadelphia, N. Little Rock, you name the place in the surrounding area and they was all sweet and we worked them. We rode on interstate 1-40 west every morning to come up with the same lick or more as the day before. This was really causing our adrenaline to flow like a river of water because we were finding real tricks like we never had before.

It's a cloudy Sunday night when Snap and I gassed up in Escatawpa to pull out on our way to Little Rock. I purchased an auto-trader magazine in search of something to buy that would better represent the type of dough (cheese) I'm clocking at this stage of the game. A Mercedes is what I had my mind set on when I came across a 240 diesel for $6,800 that I believed I could work with after a couple of new tires and a fresh paint job. It didn't matter in this era or area of living about the year model of the Benz. People and society assume if you're driving any year Benz it used more gassed than a domestic vehicle and cost more to service which gave you a little more status.

When we arrived in Little Rock it looked wet and gloomy and neither the traffic nor the people were moving at a pace which Snap and I had become accustomed. This definitely wasn't Houston or Miami. After the first day of working and scouting the surrounding area and seeing what was available for us, I placed a call to the number listed as the owner of the Mercedes in the auto trader magazine and discussed the condition and details concerning the ad and my desire to purchase the automobile. I made a counter offer and agreed to meet with the owner to purchase the Mercedes the following week.

At the end of the first week I decided to wait another week and instead sent the owner $1,000 to hold it for me one more week. My mind was made up and I had come to believe by the evidence of proof that Little Rock was going to pay for this dream car I wanted and it wasn't going to cost me the $6,500.00 out of my pocket that I had counter offered and was accepted by the owner.

We dragged the area for the next week catching good tricks for hundreds, if not thousands, of dollars for only a few to damn near no pieces of jewelry at all. I had never seen it sell the way it was selling in Little Rock. By the end of the second week with paying rent, buying weed, beer, eating and tricking-off money, I had in my pocket all the money for the Benz except maybe about $1,200.00 and called the owner to let him know I was on my way to pick it up. Snap and I made a quick stop at the Hancock Bank in Moss Point to get the remainder of the money I needed before continuing on to Pensacola where the Benz was located on Navy Blvd.

Greetings and money was exchanged and I set out to find a paint shop to remove the dull yellowish paint that was fading on my newly purchased automobile. Another twist was being brought to the game by a Coast Playa.

Chapter 34

Janice is pregnant and I'm riding my ass off from state to state. Turk, Jeff, Chuck and Mickey see the evidence of a honey hole that Snap and I have found somewhere in America but they don't know where. They asked where was we working and riding out to and I could see in their eyes that they're ready to burn the hell out of the spot as soon as I tell them where. When these guys finish with a town or city there's nothing left behind but sadness, anger and a small bank account for someone if they're working on a budget. Snap and I play it smart and decided to give them the curve and the same answer every time asked. We continued to tell them that we were working West Palm Beach.

Eventually they figured it out on their own. One misty morning when Snap and I was about to leave the room and head to work for what was going to be our last day, we hear outside that famous pimp car horn blow and peaked out the window. Guess who we see? It's Turk and the crew cussing like a soldier and screaming Bro-n-law you ain't no good, you sent us to hell while you went to heaven; you're a dirty low-down joker. Everybody is laughing because all con-men can't help but laugh when they've been conned or thrown a curve ball.

It was all in good fun and to get as much work out of a city before inviting the entire crew unless it was a major city. Snap and I tell them the spots we worked and that they can have it because we're satisfied and raised the area and kept what we have come up with.

If anyone of us ever wanted to know the whereabouts of the other or where he was working, all we had to do was ask the company that we were buying the jewelry from and where they sent the last package to that person and bingo. This is what Turk had done and the company knew we were all together because Turk was the one that plugged me in with the companies.

They rode a whole day from Palm Beach to Little Rock to get to where Snap and I was docked. We couldn't be classified as ordinary people because we wasn't thinking or doing the things that just ordinary people do. We insisted on being able to out-wit the average individual and manipulate the economical structure of society. We were Coast Playa's.

Chapter 35

Times are good for me and when I say good that's an understatement. I'm on top of the world as I know it. Everything I touch or attempt turns to gold. It seems that by me just getting up in the morning and walking out the door, I'm privileged with stumbling across money. We continued to ride back and forth to Louisiana and east over to Alabama when we're home off the road. Alabama was not such a good spot to work and was very hard to come up with some money or find a good trick. You never knew when or what you may come up with but you definitely understood the possibility of it being a hard area to come up in and if you hit a lick at all not saying a big lick you was lucky.

The game has some good days and moments where Snap and I forgot about catching a trick for money and we would get all the way off track. While working Grandbay, Alabama a country city about 10 miles east of Pascagoula/Moss Point, Ms. we had one of those days where we allow ourselves to get side-tracked. It was a memorable day where a trick female wanted the jewelry but had no money. It was another one of these days we had seen so many times where either they didn't have the money of felt it was cheaper to have sex with us to get what they wanted.

Snap and I are cruising through the back streets of the Grandbay area where there are only about fifteen-to-twenty businesses for us to ask. We're not just stuck on catching a trick inside a place of business and are also attempting to catch a moving trick passing us by. While in the process of doing what we do, we catch a Little Debbie house wife out in the yard working in her flower bed. We're rolling Hwy 90 and turn off on a dirt road in the direction of one of my father's lady friend's house. Her name is Cassy.

As soon as I make the left turn we both notice this white broad bent down pulling flowers from her front yard. I flashed the tray on her from the driver side window over Snap who is on the passenger side and she motioned for me to pull in the yard. She had on shorts with a tee-shirt tied in a knot and her hair was pinned up on her head. She wore bifocals that caused her to look nerdy.

Once I parked and got out of the car she seemed to be mesmerized by the watches in the tray. My mind went to working and I suggested we go inside. All this broad kept saying was that they was beautiful and that she would never be able to afford her husband something like this. I asked her for $1,200 for the pair of man and lady watches and she just kept sounding like a tape recorder with the same tune playing which was she couldn't afford them but wanted badly to get her husband something. She really loved this man but the thought of being able to do something nice for him had taken over her senses. Now I'm about to hint around for some sex in return for the jewelry as soon as I think of an angle that will allow me to back up if I see she's offended.

I finally work up my nerves to come right out and say we could work something out that could be our secret. She takes the bait and this broad is really into doing this for her husband. If he only knew what he had and knew that she would fuck for him to climb the ladder of success. I tell her to give me a minute and let me tell my partner what's happening and to come in because it's the both of our jewelry and he has to agreed with the deal. This is going to work the same as usually but instead of getting money we both will be paid another way by getting laid with this white broad.

She has a new born baby that's sitting in his high seat swing inside the kitchen. Snap remained in there with the baby while she and I go to the back bedroom. She takes off her glasses and lets her hair down and when she does this, I can't believe my eyes at what was hidden behind this mask. It's a beautiful white blond. I'm like got-damn and all she's saying the entire time she's falling to her knees giving me head is that she could never afford something like this for her husband any other kind of way. This shit has me fucked up because this beautiful housewife with one child that's a new born has flipped out over this fake gold. I didn't screw her because she stated her period was on or either it could have been she would have felt contaminated if she had.

When I finished with her I left the room and went in to watch the baby while Snap went in for his turn. The baby is crying his lungs out as if he knows we're abusing his mom and if he could talk daddy would surely know about these black dudes that has been with mama in the bedroom. The broad thanked us as if we had done her a world-class favor and continued to behave in a hypnotic state of mind as if none of what just happened had ever happened.

Several weeks later, I decided to pass back by the house hoping to catch her out in the yard praying she wanted to scream because what's done is done. Plus she can't tell her husband about the ordeal even if she found out she's been tricked so she's damned if she do and damned if she don't. The house is empty, curtains are down, the lawn needs mowing and the flower bed that she took so much interest in has not been attended to in a while.

I roll on by and headed up to Cassy's place to smoke a couple of joints of some good weed I had with her and kick it for a minute or two. We drank a beer while smoking and talking general talk and I asked her about the couple that lived in the house on the corner and she said that they had a serious problem that went on up there a couple of weeks ago with some black guys coming in and out of the house while the husband was at work.

The neighbors told the husband and shit erupted and it had something to do with some jewelry. I confessed to Cassy that it was me and her mouth went wide open to be covered with her hand. She said Tony, when they said something about some Jewelry my mind did not register to you but that caused a serious problem in that house. They broke up and the husband had his gun and some more stuff. The break

155

up could have been the result of the jewelry being fake or the result of her having been tainted by the Coast Playa's.

Chapter 36

I can't ignore mentioning the fact that the slummers had also been slummed before. It's funny and even maybe unbelievable but it has happened. On a early Saturday morning Chicken and I was cruising and smoking some weed. We passed through this area called Second Avenue where hustlers, crack heads, ho's and playa's hung out. You could purchase whatever you wanted on the avenue same as Carver Village. Everybody in the town and 'hoods knew us and respected us as playa's of the underworld that recognized the game.

We carried ourselves and the game like the finesse playa's we were and nobody had any reason to be intimidated about approaching us with whatever they had. We wasn't trying to kill anything we was just trying to have money and stay out of the penitentiary in whatever part of America we did our thing.

As we're cruising to a slow pace a guy flagged us down and asked was we interested in buying a set of clover leaf keystone rims and a gold bracelet. He's really talking to me as the driver and the owner of the vehicle. Both chicken and I was known but I was known as the reason for the little small center crew we had outside of Turk and the other fellows. I'm about to get them both when Chicken spoke up in the business and blurted out that he wanted the bracelet and said, damn man, if you're getting the rims let me get the bracelet. So he ended up with the bracelet and I got the rims to place on the white on white blue velour seat Regal Limited I was driving. The Benz was in the paint shop getting sprayed the color of blue and gold. I'm definitely doing it my way for a young playa. There's not another one my age at this time in this town that could match my game.

I get the rims from the guy and head straight to the tire shop to have them placed on the car. Chicken and I ride for a while longer until we decided to go our separate ways for the day. About 1:00 a.m. in the morning while I'm home in the bed with my family, I hear a car door slam and looked out the window and its Chicken walking towards the front door. That's one thing about me and my partners that didn't matter. We had no certain time that we could come by one another's house and we had become accustomed to this behavior so it wasn't a big thing to see him. I was now just wondering what was on his mind.

Janice and I are living in one of my Mom's rental houses on Grierson St. in Moss Point. I opened the door to see what was up with him this morning because like I said I wasn't going to raise any hell because it was what we did with one another. We came and called whenever the need or feelings arose to see or talk to each other.

Chicken stated he had been out gambling all night and had lost and was headed home and wanted a bag of weed.

He knew I kept a stash of good weed that I was getting from my sister-n-law Irma. She would give me this weed sometimes when I was home like I mentioned before and this had been one of those times. He had paid something like $75.00 for the bracelet and said he would let me have it for an ounce of the weed because he didn't have any more money on him at the time. I didn't think nothing of the fact that he didn't asked for it until later on in the day or for that matter just say I'll pay you later and be gone because we rolled that way with one another. Being greedy my dumb ass bit the lick while being smart mouth telling him to give it to me because he didn't want it anyway and that his greedy ass just couldn't stand to see me get both the rims and bracelet. I can't remember exactly when it was, but days later pimping Chuck woke me up to the fact that I didn't have myself nothing and that it was the new slum brass piece that was now on the market. I had not got hipped to it yet and got my ass spanked. It goes back to when you think you know it all you really know nothing at all especially in a world that's constantly changing.

It was another incident that we laughed like crazy at. One time Turk pulled up in my yard in his yellow and brown Mercedes and damn near fell to the ground getting out because of laughing so hard. He had spanked Chicken for a couple of hundred dollars with a ring. Chicken knew Turk would also come across some hell-u-va real pieces of jewelry sometimes and he thought this was one of those times. It was so funny that Turk couldn't talk for trying to tell me he spanked Chicken's fat ass. Turk said Bro-n-Law I got that fat joker good. That's how it was with us but we never did real harm to one another and kept it among ourselves like real Coast Playa.

Antonio Berry

Chapter 37

It was also during this time that one of my homeboys I grew up with also named Tony had caught a murder charge after killing another homeboy by the street name of Too-Cool. Both of these dudes were alright and it was a senseless killing from a failure to communicate. Tony's brother Bug-Kelly was running the avenue and had a club where mostly everybody on this strip hung out and this is where the murder took place.

Shortly after the murder my Buick regal was seized from me by the state of Arkansas based on a threat made good by one of the tricks. When leaving her place of business she had said, I'm going to get you Antonio if this jewelry isn't real. I had showed her my driver's license in an attempt to convince her further that the jewelry was not local.

Snap and I had worked this town called Eldorado, Ark while on our way to Little Rock. This woman had given us maybe $700.00 or $800.00 in all after I showed her my ID and she was convince the Jewelry wasn't local and she probably didn't have to worry about any local heat coming her way. After giving us the money and we're on our way out the door she remembered and had paid special attention to my name on the driver's license and said, if it's not real I'm going to get you Antonio and that fucked my head up. I damn near wanted to give her the money back but the playa in me and the trick I had made out of her wouldn't allow that to happen. These are the worst kind of tricks though because they will surely get you ran out of a city.

I hadn't noticed the fact that this was a CB pawn shop in one. Usually all these types of businesses are affiliated with the local police department some kind of way or the other. They have friends that are detectives and will stop by from time to time to check the place's books or to be given information on somebody that came through there trying to sell stolen goods or a convicted felon trying to purchase a weapon. Then it crossed my mind that this trick will never see me again and the thought of thinking about what she might or could do left my mind as fast as it came.

We decided to head that way again with Fort Smith being one of our destinations. On the way we thought what the hell we might as well try Eldorado again while on our way since the CB Pawn shop was the first place we asked and the only trick we caught in that town and it's been enough time in between for her to cool off.

I drove up Hwy 49 North as far as Jackson, MS. and Snap drove on to Ruston, LA. Before heading north to Eldorado, I pulled the license for that City out of the glove compartment to make sure we didn't have to go by City Hall to purchase another one. We still were going by the police department to check in and make them aware that we would be in the area soliciting.

Snap pulled up behind the police station which resembled a long shot gun house with a hall way straight through to the front door. Snap took the license to go in and let them know that we would be in the area going in and out of different businesses again just in case they received some calls they would know it was us and we was licensed to do what we was doing. The object was the same as before wherever we went. To keep everybody iced and especially the ones we asked that didn't buy anything.

I had a pair of 6/9 speakers in the back; the ones that use to have the removable top. While Snap is in the Eldorado Police Department checking in to let them know that we're going to be in the area, I placed the weed underneath the speaker cover so we could have something to smoke after work and on our ride up to Fort Smith.

I finished with this task and after several minutes had passed by I begin to wonder what was taking Snap so long to come out. I decided to go see for myself. I walked through the back door of the station, the same door Snap had entered and could see straight through to the other side and out the front door. As I'm walking toward the front door in an effort to determine where the dispatcher's station is, I glanced to my left and see Snap standing behind a glass partition being placed in hand cuffs and immediately turned front and center. I kept walking straight towards and out the front door. I didn't stop walking until I was in a hood where some black guys were hanging under a tree. I asked and pleaded for a ride anywhere south across the state line and into Louisiana. I explained to them that I hadn't committed a robbery or anything of the sort.

I offered a guy $30.00 to take me about 15 miles and explained my situation to him. He took and dropped me off in Ruston where I rented a motel room and called Janice while trying to sort this mess out. I had a clue and knew in the back of my mind that it was the CB/pawn shop lady that screamed. Snap had already called his Mom and she had sent a check by there to Janice for Snap's bond but that was not going to be accepted by a bondsman in Eldorado. Snap was from out of state and being charged with fraud. No bondsman was going to take such a chance. Janice sent my brother Darryl with his friends Bryant and Nunie with the cash money so we could raise Snap up out of that place.

They arrived riding in Janice's little red Escort that I had sometimes worked out of. Janice, at my request, sent some jewelry I had around the house to allow me to continue to get some work in. I couldn't allow Darryl to ride with them because not only did we have the same last name but we looked too much alike and the lady would probably swear he was me although she had read my license that said Antonio.

Snap posted bond but they would not give him my Regal Limited Edition back even though he was in control of it when he was arrested and I hadn't reported it stolen. They told him to tell Antonio to come get it. I was not stupid and said the hell with that car for a charge. It

163

had cost me but I was getting it that way and plus I had a Benz in the shop getting spray painted. The money I was getting was too much to allow an automobile to cause me to have a charge.

I never seen the car again and had a scare one time concerning the matter. One evening while passing by my Mom's house I noticed a car in the driveway with an Arkansas tag. I hurried to the phone and called to see who was in that car because it resembled a detective's Crown Victoria automobile, I called and my step-father Richard answered the phone and told me there was a insurance man in the living room talking to my Mom and my heart got back right in my chest.

A woman in Hammond, Louisiana's City Hall bought a chain one time and had the nerves to contact me by mail asking for her money back.

This was a way of life for me regardless of what one may think when it came to a person that could do this for a living and thinking it's no principle with a man that does such a thing. That is an incorrect assumption as I explained from the beginning of this story. Larceny and greed is the only way you can be a victim and without it the game won't succeed. I never conned family, friends seriously, or anybody that's known to be close to me or my family. We did each other for laughs but never to the point of harm and disrespect.

Chapter 38

It's the beginning of 1986 and time to switch the game up again to another demographic area of America. Janice is still pregnant and I decided to take her on my next mission. I rented a tow bar so I could pull her ford escort with my Benz. My plan is to work out of her escort during the day and kick it around whatever city we're in after work in the Benz.

The first place we set out to stop in is Cape Girardeau, Missouri. We're going to work the surrounding area with some of the places being the bottom portion of Illinois. It's cold and snowy some days but the motel rent has to be paid. This time it's me, Snap, Cat and Chicken. Janice is the only female. She's pregnant; quit her job which now places me as the sole provider of the family. I can handle it because I'm definitely going to find me some tricks somewhere in America, it's a must or get a job and that ain't happening for the playa.

Wasn't anything special about the Cape and nothing to really remember Missouri about except they paid on the average enough to keep you on the road.

We tried St. Louis one week and nearly starved in that big, broke, city.

We hurried up and went back down to the Cape for about two more weeks. The only thing I remember about St. Louis was at the time they had this big truck they called Big Foot sitting inside a fence out by the airport and the Cape had a reform school.

We eventually left and ventured through Evansville, Indiana and worked the days we could. Because of always being snowed in we had few days of work.

After maybe two weeks and a total of four or five days of good work we had to leave from there and find us a city where we could get some regular work in.

Sometimes you can jump out of the pot and into the fire. That's exactly what happened as we settled into Louisville, Kentucky where things took a turn for the worst all in a matter of days. Everybody is frustrated by not being able to get any serious work in and nibbling on what bank roll we have from another spot.

Louisville and St. Louis is the slowest cities I've been in; even slower than Miami. It was so slow that we weren't coming up with the rent money for the motel. When on the road you have to at least come up with rent money and money to eat even if you're not coming up with enough to send any home because if not you will end up sleeping in the car. That's just a saying because before that happens we would send home for some money through western union. It's just a figure of speech we used to place emphasis on how important it is to catch a trick and be able to stay on the road until things got better.

Snap, Cat, and Chicken had a room and the three of them are splitting the rent down the middle. Janice and I had a room but, I'm not splitting rent with anybody and have to carry the entire weight and feed two.

Every morning on our way out we stop by the front desk as always and pay rent for that day just in case we're not back by check out time. The $100.00 bills that we're busting to pay rent every morning is part of the bank roll we pulled up in this city with. Once you bust a $100.00 bill it's gone and we do this for about a week every morning.

The frustration has caused Janice and me to get into an argument one night but I can't remember the reason and with her being pregnant and going through her moods coupled with me not being able to catch a trick it didn't make matters any better. The next morning unbeknown to me she had planned and decided to leave and head home while I'm at work. A man will never know all the ways of a woman and if he tells you he does its only because he's very unlearned and inexperienced.

The next day after the morning of our argument, we pulled up from work to the motel off Interstate 65 and the Escort is gone and the Benz is parked where I left it. This particular morning we all decided to work together. My antenna immediately went up because Janice knew it wasn't smart to be riding around town in the Escort after I've been working out of that car and it would have been better to drive the Benz where she had or wanted to go.

Something didn't feel right about this scene and I had a feeling it had something to do with the argument we had and that she was still fuming about it. Don't get me wrong I knew I was a long ways from being a saint and could be difficult to live with especially when I'm not making any money the way I think I should and the way I've come accustomed to. One city would be sweet and a gold mine and the next city you could catch yourself spending the money you made in the last city to make it through. This city and St. Louis was just bad picking on my behalf. You always wanted to pick good cities after good cities in order to see your bank roll grow.

As soon as I opened the motel room door I knew immediately Janice had left. I touched the recently washed and dried clothes on the bed and they were still warm so I figure she couldn't have gone too far. Like I said before Janice was a good woman and it showed in her character because how many women after a bad argument would wash your nasty ass clothes before leaving you. I panicked and jumped in Cat's car and sped south down 1-65 doing 100 mph while checking every exit for about four or five miles acting just like Jeff did and with no luck at all and catching myself, I turned around and went back to the room. I had to stay on the road so it was a must I keep my head together. Janice told me later while we joked about it that if I had taken a certain exit I would have seen her gassing up. Nothing else had been going right for the last past couple of weeks and I guess that was just another time I couldn't pick a good exit.

I had become accustomed to Janice being on the road with me and that's what I wanted. Although I would venture out and do my thing while hanging with Snap and the fellows I always remembered she was there and it felt good being able to go back to the room knowing you had somebody there waiting.

Now I'm on the phone calling like crazy talking to Janice's sister Irma trying to see if she had called. Nobody has talked to her and I'm now thinking she must still be on the highway. My spare tire is flat in the Benz and my mind was on the possibility of my having to head towards home. It's hard for a man to try and work and worry about home at the same time and I've let myself get caught up. I didn't want to go home because my plan had been to stay on the road for three or four months but now I'm going through bull-shit that I wouldn't be if I had left Janice's ass at home the first time.

Cat and I take and drop my spare off at the tire shop and I tell the guy that we will be back in a couple of hours.

When I get back to the room Janice had made it home. We talked and she pretended that she had only left to go and see her doctor which I knew was a lie because she had never mentioned anything about an appointment and it could have very well been true. It still was an opportune time to make it seem as if it was for the argument we had and a pretext to lash out at me because of some things I had said that touched her. We talked for a minute and she stated that she would be leaving coming back after seeing the doctor tomorrow. I left it at that and will wait to straighten her ass when I see her face to face. She had it coming.

Chapter 39

We did not know that the local police in Louisville was investigating us and everybody that looked and acted suspicious. The local authorities, DEA, and the FBI were watching our room and every move we made.

 The front desk had given the authorities information that we were paying rent every morning with $100.00 dollar bills. The reason we're busting $100.00 bills is because we can't hit a lick for nothing in the world and we're spending the money we arrived in this city with.

Cat and I decided to go pick up the spare tire from the shop and we're in no big hurry because my mind is not on leaving since Janice said she's coming back to Louisville. As we're cruising puffing on a good joint of weed listening to the car stereo as if we had no care in the world, one finds us.

Minding our business, rolling through this neighborhood making our way to the tire shop in plenty of time before it closed and out of nowhere police cars come from every direction imaginable and cut right in front of me forcing me to the curb.

The cops jumped out with pistols drawn screaming for us to get out and get on the ground face down. I'm clean as a whistle in what we called back then a $120.00 Bill Crosby sweater, a pair of Stacey Adams shoes and these suckers have me and Cat face down on the ground with pistols to our heads. I'm wondering what the hell is going on because nobody has given us any real money since we've been in this city.

After they asked us a bunch of questions and getting answers that didn't coincide with what and who they were seeking, they placed us in separate cars and took us back to the room. As soon as the door opens with Cat and I standing there in hand-cuffs, the first person we see is Snap sitting on the bed with a joint in his mouth talking on the phone with some local chick he had met earlier that day. I had to actually tell Snap two or three times that these are the police, man. Snap was just too cool. So cool that he told the chick to let him call her back without him knowing what was going on.

Earlier that day, we had gotten adjoining rooms since Janice had up and left. The doors to the opposite side room were open. The cops gather us all in one room and told us how they had been watching us for a couple of days as a result of an under-cover drug buy gone bad. This was a reverse sting where one of their own was killed. They mentioned the fact that they knew Cat had bought a watch a few days ago from somebody in the projects that we frequent regularly after work to buy weed.

They mentioned these facts but that was not what they were interested in. That was small shit to them and they wanted the killers of their comrade. They wanted to make sure we had nothing to do with what transpired and wasn't involved with the other Southerners. The other Southerners were supposed to be some Florida boys. Although we were in Kentucky, they considered us Southern folks.

Two of them were searching the other room when one of them suddenly holla out, whose suit case of weed and pistol is this in the closet? We all screamed and answered at the same time in synchronization, not ours. Things have calmed down with them believing now that we truly don't know or have anything to do with what has happened in their city with the killing of a police officer.

The end result was only with me going to jail because of this bull-shit younger cop had already called in about the joint of weed I had been smoking when they threw down on us curb-side and I couldn't get rid of it. As soon as he done it the older cop responded a little upset about him calling in on something so small with them being on a larger mission and this ended up being unrelated to their investigation. He didn't like the fact that they had to go through the paper work about a lousy joint of weed for their efforts in trying to bring in some dangerous criminals. He was upset about the young cop's decision to call it in.

I set in jail in a holding tank until the next morning waiting to see a judge because Kentucky was a common wealth state and a Judge had to be the one that set your bond. Not like Mississippi where the desk clerk at the station tells you what its going to cost for you to leave up out of their jail. This tank was filled with winos and smelled terrible.

Bond was set the next day and I was immediately released with Snap and the rest waiting outside for me to come through the door. This incident transpired simply because we were stereotype-profiled to the supposedly trained eye. I guess we did and could have passed for a couple of drug dealers but the game allowed you to ride and dress that way as I stated before.

Janice made it back and after I straightened her we decided to pack up and get the hell out of Kentucky. I wasn't going to leave without a phone book. This will help me to find an attorney I can hire that could represent me with not having to be there. I hope to never have to or have any reason to ever return to Kentucky.

Our eyes and the front ends of our vehicles are pointed in the direction of Knoxville, Tennessee by way of Lexington, Kentucky and then 1-75 South. Knoxville, we're about to bring it to you with no mercy so get ready. Here comes the Coast Playa's.

Antonio Berry

Chapter 40

1-40 and Ashville Highway in Knoxville, Tennessee is where we rented a motel room with easy access on and off the interstate. This was a convenient spot with a Waffle House being directly across the street for us to grab breakfast first thing in the morning. In some of these cities we would become such a regular patron until we would develop a relationship with the employees. Within the first couple of days being there Snap, Cat and Chicken had tricked some broads to come by the room for some drinks and to smoke some weed.

I always played it close even with Janice being on the road with me. I would often visit Snap and them and party with whomever they had in there room as if Janice wasn't a few doors down or on the other side of the building. I would even have sex or get some head on some occasions. This city was full of massage parlors which was nothing but legalized prostitution businesses on another level. I've gotten oral sex more times than I can remember in one of these establishments, or just sex. A couple of the females I had spoken with said that their husbands or boy-friends had no idea what they were really doing for a living and tips. They actually thought their woman was rubbing a customer's back and legs. They were rubbing his third leg. See, a man could never know all the ways of a woman and would end up being a trick every time if he's not firm in his game.

Cat had met this broad whose mom owned a ludicrous beauty parlor in the hood and the broad Cat met drove a two door coupe convertible Benz. Cat always had a way of coming up good when it came to catching worthy broads.

Snap had found a buddy named Jam Boogie and they were spending their time hanging out with their new friends. Cat's girl had some girl friends that she would bring around every now and then and brighten up the party for Snap, Chicken and even myself at times. We all had come to be pretty cool with one another. Cat and Chicken had paired off and was riding everyday to this city west of Knoxville called Cookeville. They were riding miles out every morning and were beating Snap and me back in and we was working local. Knoxville wasn't bad but the town of Cookeville was being extremely sweet to Cat and Chicken until they begin to call it Cocksville.

Snap and I came to the conclusion that we might have better luck hitting a big lick if we rode out everyday same as Cat and Chicken. They was hitting licks like $700.00 to $800.00 daily and back before lunch so it had to be as soon as they exit off the interstate and the first person they asked had to be paying them. We eased the conversation in to them about us riding with them the next morning and they accepted our gesture and said it was no problem. No sooner than we had asked a couple of joints, I run into a place that had just recently opened.

The owners of this swim suit shop were two good-looking white females and they were taking the bait. They were mesmerized by the glitter like most tricks and asked that famous question. What do I want for it? They were saying that they had just purchased some inventory for the store and really didn't have any spare money. If not for that they would give me what I'm asking. They never took their eyes from the tray and I'm thinking that maybe they don't want me to get the impression that they have any money in the store in case I am a robber.

By this time along in the conversation Snap had done walked in and we begin putting down on the two together. We informed them that we had a shit load of this stuff and are trying to get rid of it for a reasonable price and for twenty grand they can have it all. So now I collect pieces from everybody in an attempt to get us all a piece of this money if they let any of it leave their hands. All the pieces are laid out before them and we finally agree on a figure of $13,000.00 and I'm playing the role of the victim in this deal by letting them have it this cheap. Ok, I say, give me the $13,000.00 and I hope you are willing to buy from me again if I come through.

This day we're riding in my Blue Benz, four deep and when we get in to pull off to follow the two broads to the bank for the money, a shit load of police cars comes from everywhere and threw down on us like we had robbed a bank. I show them the business license and receipt for the jewelry order and they still told us to follow them to the police station down town. Once we're there they placed us in a holding cell until they could run a nationwide check on everybody. A detective came to the bars and asked which one of us asked those women for $20,000.00. I scream and I screamed loud, $20,000.00 we can't get $20,000.00 for the jewelry and the car together so ain't nobody asked them for no $20,000.00. Damn, now I'm thinking these white folks may try to case us up for fraud with these tricks testimony. They're probably really upset now that they have been made aware of the scheme we were attempting to run on them with some fake jewelry. I could see the looks on their faces in a supposed to be blind justice court room.

This heat we're under is the direct result of somebody in the crew failed to properly ice another business before leaving out the door after showing them the tray of jewelry. Another business in the area sees four black men coming in and out of different businesses in the area and called the police trying to be a Good Samaritan. That's why it's very important to ice the person that don't bite or buy and just looks because the trick next door may be in there paying your partner until the cops show up and the trick is blown. Even if the trick gives you a bad feeling, never come to where your partner is. Always make the trick think you've left the area. That way the cops won't be snooping around in that vicinity.

After keeping us in the holding cell for almost four hours, they finally release us but not without telling us we better not stop for gas until we're miles out of their city and county with this bull-shit we're trying to do. We did just what they asked and went somewhere else fast. They slipped a little though because they didn't say we had to leave the state or bring in the troopers same as Carolina did. Carolina escorted us all the way across the state line. On the way in we worked a small town named Lebanon trying to get rent money after blowing a complete day and blowing two tricks for maybe $13,000.00 and with it were run out of town.

Bristol, Johnson City, Kingsport, all was in our eye sight to drag with a net. They would not be looked over. We dragged these East Tennessee cities for two or three weeks and didn't have under a $300.00 to $400.00 day which allowed us to continue to keep our feet out of the penitentiary. That's something these Coast Playa's was definitely trying to do.

Chapter 41

It was cool in the mornings and nice and warm in Knoxville by mid-afternoon. We're cruising, scouting out the joints trying to find a honey nest in Sevierville, Tennessee when we spot this two door blue convertible Benz in a parking space designated for the manager at this motel. This was a tourist area in Tennessee where Dolly Parton was famous and the scenery was rich. I pulled in and walked to the counter where a short mid-twenties blond female was working as the receptionist. I asked her was the boss in and although reluctantly, she directed me towards the door that said manager and at the same time had the look in her eyes and body language that said what in the hell could these vermin possibly want with her boss.

From where I was positioned I could see an older sexy almost completely white headed woman behind the glass window at a desk talking on the phone. I get her attention by opening up the tray so she could see it from behind the glass and two seconds later she was hanging up the phone and gesturing for me to come in. I gently opened the door real humbly with the tray in the open position so boss would know immediately off the bat that I didn't have a pistol or anything like that, come to take or rob her of anything and only had something to sell to her.

People would still occasionally and probably most of the time because they don't know you sometimes would be afraid of you even though you're doing your best to show them and its apparent you came to sell as opposed to taking. Their mind is still trying to figure out what type of person you are to just walk in their place of business in the first place and whether or not you have actually stolen this stuff you have in your hand. It use to be so funny to watch them act fidgety with you knowing in your mind you hadn't stolen anything or had no intentions to harm anybody. You would be very mentally aware of their thoughts.

We talked for about fifteen minutes going back and forth with figures until we finally agreed on one. Boss Lady stated that she had to go to the bank in order to get the money because she didn't have that type of cash lying around for petty cash. By this time Snap had came in and I explained the deal with Boss Lady and that she was going to give me $1,500.00 but she first had to take a trip to the bank which I said wasn't a problem. Snap pulled up on her and they also went back and forth until they agreed on a price for the pieces he had and we had what we thought was a solid deal.

She stated the bank was a couple of blocks up the street and it would only take her ten minutes and asked could we wait in the lounge area. She informed her receptionist that she will be back shortly. Unbeknown to us at the time, Boss Lady had pulled a fast one that got by us because we was so caught up in thinking about the money and that she was a good trick and missed it. As we set there with more than ten minutes already passed, something told me to walk out side and look towards the direction of the bank and see if I could notice Boss Lady or her Benz on its way back. Bam, I notice the two-door Benz pulled in a parking space at the bank about two blocks away in a bank parking lot as she said it was. I was looking to see when Boss Lady would walk out the door to the car when all of a sudden out of no where a police car pulled up right next to her Benz. This didn't look good and may not play out well and I wasn't about to take a chance. It could have just been a coincident but I wasn't taking the chance that it was. You win some you lose some but in this game you won more than you lost and this was going to be a small loss.

I flipped into paranoia mode and eased hurriedly back in to let Snap know what I had just seen and for us to make a fast exit based on this sighting. I check the tray I still had in my pocket and low and behold this slick old broad had done cuffed a ladies ring from the tray on me.

Shit, we have to make a move and get out of here fast because cops may be on their way. It could be that her husband is a police and he's dirty and buy stuff and she just may have cuffed it to make sure that if I do leave she had the piece she wanted. Whatever the reason, I was not about to take the chance for a $2.50 ring.

The suspicious nature in me tells me it's not good and to rise from this spot. I know I should watch the building from a distance but I'm not familiar with this part of the country or their hospitality concept. I politely tell the receptionist to let Boss know not to go anywhere and that we will be right back and had to make a run up a few blocks. We got the hell out of there and messed up in the process of doing that. I don't know what the hell I was thinking about when I took off but I went in the wrong direction and headed for Gatlinburg not knowing there was one way in and one way out. This direction took us straight up into the Smokey Mountains. Shit, there is no way out except to try and ease out through as much of the back side as we can and stay off the main drag as much as possible until we reach 1-40 and get our butts back to Knoxville as fast as possible and chalk this one up to the game.

We still couldn't avoid Boss Lady's business establishment and it looked quite. We avoided traveling directly in front of it. It looked clear so maybe it was good. I'd rather live without knowing than to have a case. The Coast Playa lives another day.

Antonio Berry

Chapter 42

The only two cities we were run out of in Tennessee while working that state was Cookeville and Oak Ridge. We decided we would meet the UPS man at the office and get our box before the truck began its route. We knew if we waited that we wouldn't receive our ordered package until sometime around noon and this didn't set good with us if we was going to try and catch a trick and be back at the room by noon puffing on some good weed. We were able to catch the truck at the office and pay for our boxes and be on our way.

The boxes were around $275.00 a piece and we're going to have to take all of our jewelry to work with us; something we didn't care to do. The room was too far in the opposite direction to drop half of it off. All it usually took was two trays at the most with a couple of extra rings and chains to meet your quota of satisfaction.

Our destination this morning is Oak Ridge, Tennessee. The City Hall informed us that we wouldn't need to purchase a license as long as we were going to go business to business and not to any residents. We began our journey of in and out of the different businesses. Evidently someone we iced didn't believe the ice cap we left them with and still called the local authorities.

The cops pulled us over asking for our ID's and what were we doing in their city. We explained that the jewelry was ordered from a company out of California and City Hall said as long as we were going to go from business to business we didn't need a permit. The dispatcher was informed that we would be in this area. One smart red neck said to let him take a look at the jewelry and in my mind I'm thinking for what? Had somebody recently been spanked in this area or does he know the game? It turned out he knew the game.

This cock-sucker-tobacco-chewing-red-neck is turning the jewelry over in his hand and looking at the back where the numbers are. The numbers read like 14kt36079 so that the 14kt wouldn't stick out or be obvious for other reasons. He asked what did these numbers mean and we told him those numbers was nothing but model numbers for placing an order describing the type of watches you wanted to purchase. He asked me if I thought he was a fool. Oh shit!! I'm really thinking now here's a tough one that we're going to have to play the head game with. No Sir I don't think that but it's the truth. I tell you what he said, we're going to keep this shit and ask you to leave our city and never come back over here with this bull-shit again or I can take you down town and arrest you for the investigation of fraud due to trying to pass this shit off as gold. We lost again. They took both Snap and my entire box we had just got out that morning and now we didn't have anything to work with.

You know, we had mastered this game of short con and couldn't be and refused to be stopped. We found the first Jr. Food Mart and purchased four Eseiko's watches for like $80.00 at $20.00 each. We then took a toothpick and some rubbing alcohol and took the E off and had Seiko and sold all four of them for $60.00 to $70.00 a piece and placed an order before sun down to come in the next day. This way the loss wouldn't seem that big of a deal and we were going to definitely make some trick pay. When it came to con and counterfeiting, I had played it from buying a 59¢ bottle of cake decorations from Winn Dixie and removing the orange dots to sell them for sunshine acid to making homemade hashish. It was in our repertoire to get money like a Coast Playa.

Chapter 43

We have now been docked in Knoxville for two months and its getting close for Janice to have the baby. She is getting on my last nerve with her crankiness by the day and it's about to drive me crazy. I love her but, it's about to become intolerable to be around her. The Attorney I chose from the phone book took care of the case in Kentucky and had it dismissed and it was no longer hanging over my head. It was constantly on my mind about what these common wealth red necks might do for an out-of-towner showing up in their Court Room about any kind or amount of dope.

After about almost four months on the road and some very sweet times, I believe its due for us to head towards home for some mind relaxation and work on coming back out fresh. If for no other reason, so, that Janice can further prepare herself for the soon to be coming day of delivery.

Our baby girl Tara is born on July 8, 1986 and Janice is spending time at the house while I continue to ride the highway and do my thing. I never missed a beat and was able to actually concentrate better. I would sometimes fly her and Tara to the state I happened to be in and working. Tara was spoiled rotten and was eating table food at only a few months old and looked every bit of it. We thought she was going to have a problem with growing some hair one time because for a while only a patch would grow directly in the center of her head. Janice was placing her in every ball and contest that was hosted in town. I had her counting to ten as soon as she was able to say her first word.

I had taught her how to walk so quickly until some people had begin to say that she was making room for another baby. That was furthest from the truth and our mind at least my mind anyway.

At night she would cry and when I was home off the road, I would let Janice sleep while I get up and make Tara a bottle, walk her around and rock her back to sleep or whatever it took to quiet her down.

Whenever we would travel the road with friends and their children, we could give them all money to go in the store to buy something and while the other children would buy candy and chips, Tara would head straight for the sausage, biscuit or pizza freezer. She wanted something real to eat and could eat. Janice's sister Irma had Tara spoiled also but Tara knew how to make Irma so mad that she would turn red. Irma had always bought Tara expensive dresses and gave her something every chance she got or when she would see her. Tara could turn so cold blooded on her sometimes until it made me feel bad at moments. It was amazing to see a child so young with so much sense and ability. Irma would ask Tara for some candy or whatever she may have at the time and Tara would flat out with no hesitation tell Irma no as if go to hell. It used to be kind of funny because Tara wouldn't bend no matter what Irma did for her. Irma would go ballistic and say heifer I'm not buying you shit else and Tara would respond with so, my daddy will buy it.

One day we were in Irma's restaurant and Tara asked for a soda and Irma told her no and asked where her money was. Tara stuck her lips out and turned around to me and said daddy give me a dollar. These two was a trip. Tara had always been grown for her age but not a bad baby and nobody ever had a problem with keeping her.

I drank moderately and Janice didn't drink alcohol at all unless we was on vacation and she then would sometimes have a sip of something light like a fruit drink mixed with a little alcohol. We sometimes kept wine or other alcoholic beverages in the refrigerator for guests that may come over to the house. The contents of one bottle gradually continued to evaporate and we couldn't figure out why to save our souls. I had even accused Janice of sipping on the low and she swore up and down it wasn't her. One day I finally put two and two together and it hit me. Tara kept wetting the bed so I called her in the house and told her she better not lie to me. I said Tara have you been drinking out of that bottle of wine in the refrigerator? She burst out and started to cry and said yeah. I told her I wasn't going to spank her because she told me the truth but she better not do it again and get out of here and go play. Tara had been floating around the house on cloud nine with nobody having a clue and probably had figured out what the wine was doing to her and wanted more. Now tell me that wasn't too much sense.

I made a super special effort to assure that all my children knew one another and it wasn't a thing about half sisters or brother no, it was just plane sisters and brother. Janice and I would take them on vacation and shopping sprees together all the time. Meeka and Tara had even traveled to the Caribbean Islands. They had go-carts, four wheelers, bikes, dogs, fish aquariums, computers from Radio Shack, stereo's, TV's in their own rooms and all the latest clothes fashion any child could dream for. They even had a large Amazon talking bird name Freeman that cost me $3,500. They had the first eight ball jackets that came out or hit the town. They had them before the grown folks. They stayed fresh and nobody would or could dispute the fact that I did good by my children. Whether it was taking and picking them up from the private school or when they would call and tell me to bring some money to the school for their book fair.

The school would sometimes call and say they was having problems with little Tony and I'd make a surprise visit to the school without him knowing. They would sometimes call and tell me to either pick them up in one of the Benz's, Jag, '64 Chevy, '68 Chevy or the convertible - whichever one they wanted to show off for their friends in that morning. Some people said I was spoiling them too much but I called it showing love and allowing them to enjoy it along with me; like a Coast Playa.

Chapter 44

Nothing has changed in the flow of my money and the selling of slum jewelry except I'm beginning to catch myself venture into some things I really didn't know was some real dangerous waters while trying to continue to slum at the same time. These dangerous waters are pulling me strong and it's hard to resist. Our riding has slowed down tremendously and I'm taking whoever I can when Darryl was not available due to him having now entered college. Snap has let that bad gorilla begin to pull him in another direction. It had also begun to pull me but for other reasons that was green. My mind was strictly on getting paid.

I did my damndest to encourage Darryl to stay in school and continue his education but he kept insisting that he wanted to ride the road and travel with me to sell slum jewelry. He had tasted the blood of the slum game like a pit-bull taste's its prey. To help try and convince him with the rational I was explaining about staying in school, I would let him take my Benz or whatever vehicle he wanted to school with him hoping that he would remain there. I use to even make sure he kept a pound or two of weed - the best grade - around so he could keep extra money in his pocket and to give him that hustling feeling. This wasn't as exciting to him as the road game of slumming. The last thing I needed was for Mama to be on my back again and blaming me for Darryl dropping out of college. All I could think about was how Mama would act a big fool with me if this boy quit school and hit the road with me. It would probably give her a heart attack to see her baby boy now following my footsteps.

Darryl decided he was going to quit regardless after taking a short break at the house. This was done with the belief in his mind that he was going to ride with me when I left town. I asked him was he crazy or just plain stupid. I told him Mama would blow a stack so hell no he's going to have to get him a job and deal with this on his own because this was one that I was going to stay out of. He hung around and searched for a job in order to let Mama realize it wasn't my plan for him to quit school just so he could run behind me and that I had nothing to do with his decision. Hell no, this was her baby boy we're talking about and plus my stepfather Richard had Darryl spoiled rotten. This was a big disappointment to Richard that he had quit school. Mama had already disapproved of what I was doing and thought I should bring my butt off the road and stay home with my family and find a job and live what she considered a decent life.

I finally thought enough time had elapsed for Darryl to be hanging around the house doing nothing. It seemed as if he wasn't even trying to get or wanted a job. I chose to take him with me thinking this would be better than him eventually finding trouble. At first Darryl was only riding with me during his summer breaks. I can honestly say he was able to execute the game pretty good and actually better than some I tried to give this game to. The student again is a reflection of their teacher and this would be the beginning of the regular road traveling for Darryl and his sole income. He would seek to become another slum hustler and live the life that it brings.

I'm lying on the couch one afternoon watching a football game trying to relax and enjoy being home off the road. Janice and the children are out somewhere giving me some peace and much needed solitude. I suddenly hear a knock on the door and get up to check it out because I hadn't heard a vehicle. I looked out to open the door to a guy we called Willie. Willie went into detail explaining to me that my buddy Chicken is in the car stressed out to the point of suicide and has been up all night crying from a broken heart. Chicken's long-time off and on girlfriend had abandoned him in the middle of the night out of the blue to marry a Navy soldier and left the country for Germany before he was able to realize what was happening. Chicken had not seen this coming from his blind side. I stepped a little further out on the front porch and told him to get out of the car and come into the house and tell Willie he could leave that I have it from here.

In an attempt to ease Chicken's pain and take the ordeal off his mind, I planned a trip for us to leave as soon as possible to hit the road with a box of slum. Chicken, Darryl, Me and another guy that I don't associate with today, because I don't associate with about 90% of the fakers and could care less if they fell from grace and off the face of the earth. We ride down to Florida again and work around Orlando, St Pete, Fort Myers and Tampa area before deciding to take it in to the house. When we do decide to head for the house it's those dangerous waters that cross our minds again. The work as we called was cocaine and it seemed like a good harmless idea to take back home for some fast extra cash and that's exactly what we did. It wouldn't have been a bad idea if it had been controllable but it wasn't. The addiction to money could be just as strong as the addiction to the drug.

Now I've created myself a habit with the intentions of riding out only to be gone for a week or two. I'm only interested in working long enough for enough money to purchase some more cocaine and bring it back home. I believe I've got myself something better than selling slum and have gravitated towards it in the most aggressive manner.

On a particular trip we take two broads from the house with us one name Diane and the other Sherry. Jacksonville, Florida was our point of interest to dock and slum for a minute. I did this with the idea of it being added therapy for Chicken trying to get his heart back healthy and plus the women could do their thing which was prostitute while we slum. Diane was a down red-bone broad who was very impressed at how we played the game different from the way she was introduced to it and shown to play by a crew she once ran with. The dude's that introduced her to the game of slumming was more of a street corner type of slummers and was on some other type of foolishness for

189

instance getting high. They would ride into a city and the first thing they would seek is the blocks where the hustlers hung out and tried only to trick the dope boys out of their work.

I first take Sherry on the road and bring Diane after one of my weekends rush home to get rid of some cocaine I had purchased. Diane and I rode all the way to Jacksonville talking and chopping it up. We never turned on the radio the entire drive which was about six hours. I was on some mack time and didn't think one minute about sex because there was going to be plenty of time for that type of action.

I had a plan and it was to get paid and that was my focus. The plan was that once I catch a good trick and he paid me I would have the broads give them the go-go eyes and get the trick aroused with their body and suggestive dressing. If they bit for the slum the chances were good they would turn a trick with the broad and it would be a win/win situation all the way around.

Sherry was a different story and personality than Diane and Sherry was a bad head ache to be bothered with. I did not and was not running behind any broad, especially a mud-kicker.

Darryl and the other dude that I don't associate with would ride to Miami and pick up the small amount of work we was getting at the time and bring it to Jacksonville. Once they make it there, Chicken and I would take it back home to sell while they remained there in Jacksonville slumming. I had left Sherry with them with the instructions that she was to pay the motel rent for them every day and that was all I wanted her to do until I made it back to town which would only be a couple of days. When I make it back with Diane in the car with me after the six hours of riding and talking, Darryl informed me that he hadn't seen Sherry since five minutes after I pulled off and she hadn't paid rent for a single day. They had worked St. Augustine and other surrounding areas and had caught some good tricks that kept them going and giving them a small bank roll.

Within twenty minutes of Diane and me exiting off 1-95 South onto Phillips Highway in Jacksonville and into the parking lot of the first motel to the right which was the Econo Lodge guess who pops up? Sherry pops her butt up looking like something from the Tales of the Crypt and smelling like sewage. This hooker looks as if she has been smoking crack day in and day out non-stop since I been gone. Janice probably didn't and I was 100% sure she didn't know I had any broads on the road with me and I wasn't about to have this hooker's death on my hands and the word gets out and back to Janice that she was with me. Not this dude, I had more sense than that. I found the nearest Greyhound bus station and loaded Sherry on it and stayed there until it pulled off heading toward Moss Point/Pascagoula Mississippi. This hooker could cost me a case and more than she was worth and that I didn't need. It was Bye Sherry to this Coast Playa.

Chapter 45

If you can believe it, I've now gravitated so much at this point toward running in and out of town with cocaine until I have damn near set the slum game aside as if it never existed. Not only have I purchased another Benz but, a Jaguar, a blue Seville, a turquoise Lincoln Versailles and a couple of Motorcycles. I'm having a quick change in the flow of my money, material items, women and it's all coming too fast. It has caused me to become lazy in not having to get up and flat foot hustle or travel the road in search of a trick. My only reason for traveling these days is to find a connection and good prices for the cocaine. The money is coming and coming fast.

I hooked up with a guy in Miami named Yogi who became a very long-time good friend and still is today. With him and his people it was a never ending supply. Some of the playa's in the dope game around my home town was upset with the power move I was making and was screaming like I had done something foul because of how far down and cheap I had caused the prices of ounces of cocaine to become. Ounces went from $1,200 and $1,500 to $900.00 and $750.00 over night and my response to all this ranting was, I can get this stuff like water so get with it or move out of the way for a real hustler trying to get paid.

After a very short time of getting down real seriously with the dope game than I had been with the slum game for a while and with the money piling up; it now had me paranoid. I decided it would be best for my family and me to move to a different location not only to duck the authorities but the would-be robbers.

The place I chose was Orlando, Florida. It wasn't too slow or too fast and you could ride with out-of-state tags and not be harassed by the local police. There were always plenty of tourists around and it made it that much easier to live there. I would sometimes bring all my children and some of their cousins there for maybe a month at a time during the summer.

I remember once having my children, nieces and nephews down there for a trip to Disney World. This day it was raining outside like a rain forest. The children was running around and screaming Uncle Tony Uncle Tony turn the T.V. off its lighting outside. I got smart mouth with the children and told them to sit their butts down somewhere and that it was my T.V. and if lighting hits it I will buy another one. It was less than twenty seconds after I said that statement when lightning struck and hit nothing but the T.V. Those children laughed at me until they cried like crazy. From that day on to now, I don't play with lighting. When it starts I get my butt somewhere and sit down out of the way.

While living in Orlando I continued the habit of taking cocaine back to Mississippi as if it was legal. Jeff had called one day and said for me not to come that way because they was picking up everybody left and right on secret indictments. They had been issued and served and the jump out boys was every where. The helicopter was flying the neighborhoods and I didn't know if my name was on one of those indictments. We had done made that area cocaine heaven and people were coming from as far as New Orleans, Mobile, Pensacola and Tallahassee to purchase for the prices we had. It was cheaper for a person to come from Tallahassee and pay $750.00 and a three hour ride than ride to Miami and pay $500.00 for an eight or nine hour ride. So I thought it would be smart to sit my butt settled for a minute until I could figure out what the hell was going on because some more hustlers I knew that was moving cocaine had been picked up. They had even arrested Jeff but it was the state and he had enough money to take care of any state charges including a murder if there was any doubt.

I stayed away from Mississippi for six months and would not cross the state line for a funeral. Mobile, Alabama was as far as I would come and allowed a few people from Mississippi to come over there and get cocaine from me. Trinity Garden was the first place I ever just hung out in Mobile. My crew and I was getting so much money that I felt like a fool to have been this close to this city for so long and just discovering what it had to offer. Now that I have discovered it I have no plans to leave anytime soon. Not this Coast Playa.

Mobile, Alabama had become my place of destination when pulling out from Orlando and heading up the road with a package of cocaine. Mobile was sweet and probably hard to believe for anyone who hadn't been there that a hustler could become a millionaire over night. I hustled in Mobile for nine months straight without letting up. Most people there thought we was Florida boys and never associated us with Mississippi. The authorities had finally become the reason for me leaving there in a hurry and not returning for a couple of years.

I'd seen hundred-thousand dollar days many times. The local hustlers would buy anywhere from ten to twenty or more ounces at a time for the prices of $800.00 to $1,000 and they thought that was giving it away. They had been paying much more for so long that they couldn't believe it and some thought it was a game.

Hustlers in Mobile were regularly seen in the Moss Point/Pascagoula area during this era to purchase cocaine and weed. It was also a time when Mississippi hustlers would ride to Mobile for the same because that's where everything was once also. Everybody had their times in the game from the West Coast to the East Coast.

Coming to Mobile and constantly living in motels was getting old and subject to bring unnecessary heat from the authorities and the added attention that I neither wanted nor would be good for what I was doing. I found an Apartment out in West Mobile in a complex named Norwood that wasn't too far once I exited off I-10 in Tillsman Corner. It was large, quiet and gave me the feel of being a local. I would bring females to spend the night and some would even come by to clean and to check on things when I wasn't in Town. Three of my favorite locals were Sheree, Paula and Stephanie and they hung around us more than any other females.

Somebody had constantly continued to cut the antenna wire to the police scanner I had set up in the apartment. It wasn't long before the culprit was finally revealed. Janice, the children, and I had came home for the Easter holiday and she had taken them to Mississippi to spend some time with our families and their cousins before we headed back home to Florida. They hadn't been seeing their cousins regularly anymore and it was a good trip for them. This particular morning I wanted to get the tires on my Lincoln balanced and rotated before we got back on the highway to Orlando. The Sport rims cause this to be needed more than it would have with the factor rims.

Janice was going to follow me to Goodyear on Airport Blvd. to drop the Lincoln off and take me back to the apartment before she went to Mississippi to pick up the children and some money. When we pulled out of the complex of Norwood a load of undercover and unmarked cars came from everywhere with pistols. They was beating on my back window telling me to stick my right arm out the window, take my left arm and put the car in park and turn off the engine. My windows were dark all around the car and they couldn't see inside.

They took us to the FBI building down town and held us there for several hours with one arm hand cuffed to the chair while a serious check for warrants was made on all of us. This agent I was sitting in front of had taken his pistol and placed it on the desk before my face as if he thought I was a damn fool and would reach for it. I was wondering what the hell was going through his mind because wasn't anything illegal found and I had no reason to fear being charged for a crime. They seized Darryl's white Cadillac that a white man auto dealer had reported he paid cash for and he had put about $10,000 in music in it. I had hid $3,000 in a phone box one night in the closet and had forgotten it was there after bringing this broad home one night and didn't want to get clipped. I was drunk but not too drunk to be a fool about my money. After hours of the bull-shit they released us to serve as a serious warning that I intended to heed.

I quickly changed my mind and said that's it. I'm through with Mobile and if I made it without a case coming up as a result of this investigation, then there won't be one, not on me.

We needed some traveling money and since we had to pick the children up in Mississippi we were going to kill two birds with one stone. Our plan was to do exactly that, ride to Mississippi, pick up Meeka, Tara and some money and head home to Orlando.

On the way to Mississippi and traveling west on I-10, a blazer pull alongside my Lincoln and it appeared that somebody with a light on was in the back looking down in our vehicle trying to determine the occupants. I immediately pulled off on the next exit which was the dog track exit and made a u-turn and headed back in the opposite direction which was now east on I-10 trying to get across the Florida line as soon as possible. I thought about just stopping in Pensacola to borrow a few dollars from Turk until we made it to Orlando. I'd call Darryl later to bring the children on down for us. Turk was nowhere to be found and probably wasn't even in town. I had only hoped that we didn't have car problems

When we made it to Orlando the next morning to the Windover Health Club where we were living, before I would enter the house as a matter of fact the parking lot, I dropped Janice off so she could walk there and trash the triple beam scales, hot pistol, bags, beakers and baking soda. Anything remotely associated with dope I wanted it out of the house. It was over for me.

Chapter 46

The school year was about to come to an end for the children in Orlando and the beginning of the summer vacations. Meeka had completed a full year at Richmond Height Elementary. The episode in Mobile had Janice and I discussing other options for a source of income while trying to hold on to what we had gained. We talked about the possibility of moving back to Mississippi and opening up a small neighborhood convenience store with a deli. Janice was good and very business orientated and was knowledgeable about this type of business. With her experience and my savvy, we couldn't fail.

We agreed on a plan and packed up to move knowing home will always be home and the best place for us to settle down. People will talk that crazy talk about home but the first place they go in hard times is back where they started which is home. Time wasn't hard for us by no stretch of the imagination but I was looking for a way out of what I thought might become a serious problem.

The store was opened and named after Lameeka and Latara, (L & L Groceries). I was trying hard to keep my hands clean from the street life and had actually succeeded doing it for an entire year. I acquired a habit that had me spending money too fast with nothing coming in and just living off what I had saved.

The store was only keeping itself open and hadn't yet begun to substantially profit. It may pay one or two bills at the house at the most. Beyond that there was nothing to brag about concerning our decision to open this business. The store was not able to keep the vehicles serviced, buy groceries for the house, clothes or medical for the family and the smart thing to do would have been to sell the vehicles. The store done absolutely nothing for the pockets and I mean nothing. It sure couldn't help afford with the weed habit I had a taste for.

After beating my brains out trying to stay afloat with giving the store a chance to pick up, I was torturing myself trying to leave the cocaine game alone. What was making the store slow during this era was a particular fad that was out and it was about not being a two stopper. I didn't have gas pumps and the store a few blocks away did. So a person would be more inclined to stop where they could get what they wanted to eat, drink and gas at the same place. I had to do something and do it fast.

I stepped to Darryl and another dude and asked them about trying our hand at the road again with slumming before picking that package of cocaine up again. I wasn't ready to throw bricks at the penitentiary again and be going nowhere in a hurry. Everybody agreed and was ready to do something because they to was feeling the crunch. It was even harder for them than me and I had a family but they were younger and running the streets and somewhat still living a life of a playa.

I ordered us a package of jewelry in preparation for this journey. The package arrives and now we're ready to hit the road in search of some victims like we use to do back in the days. The same as when we were bringing the game to an end we decided to try our hand again with two females on the road. Their names this time were Germaine and Mary and their purpose wasn't the same as the previous females. We had them for some in house fun once we were off work. Germaine was for me and Mary was for one of the other three partners. No it wasn't Darryl.

Chapter 47

I'm now struggling in the slum game and believe it's only because my heart isn't in it as before and it's not panning out as before. Something was definitely wrong. It was as if the game had a mind of its own and was telling me that I had been disrespectful to it after all the years it allowed me to eat and live well. This is what appeared to be happening because I couldn't catch a decent trick nor did I have the patience as before, which was necessary to be able to hang in there waiting for one to finally come through for me.

Damn, the slum game was trying to press me into picking the package of cocaine up or choose between the two knowing I refuse to be broke or even think of that possibility. I'm now thinking about how much longer I can live with no income and continue riding in a Benz, Jag, Cadillac and a Lincoln. I actually know I won't be able to do it too much longer and might as well accept the fact that I need to sell some of the material items I accumulated while pushing the cocaine and stop living above my means. The dope game is over for me is what I had thought.

Opening L&L Groceries had cost me almost one hundred thousand dollars and I'm still spending trying to establish it as a prominent profitable business. I surely cannot see me earning my money back and have almost accepted the fact that it was a bad investment. All indications seem to be just that, a bad investment. Janice loves it and she's in her element. The store is giving Janice another meaning and purpose in life but for me its beginning to be depressing.

It would be years later after I have gotten everything back on track and stacked another bank roll that I would see the pimp guy from North Carolina named Green-Eyes again. He was not presented in the best of light and circumstances. The beast and the gorilla of all which had taken so many playa's out of the game had found its way into Green-Eyes life. It had not only taken him by surprise but for the ride of his life.

He's now riding hoping to put down whatever and wherever he can in order to put some money in his pocket. He's no longer pimping and it's seemed to be the other way around. He has a couple of pieces of slum jewelry he's trying to sell. His traveling ended him in Pensacola, Florida where some locals recognized the game he was playing and sent him in the direction of the master of the game, Turk. Turk at this time is still slumming and had a clothing store called TGIF (Thank God It's Friday). Turk was known to the locals as the slum king and whenever a conversation or doubt would come up concerning the game of slumming, Turk was the man to go to. He would even sometimes give different guys pieces of jewelry to sell and point them in the direction of an area that might be good to get paid.

Green-Eyes and Turk had been carrying on a conversation for a about thirty minutes discussing the ins and outs of the game when all of a sudden Green-Eyes mentioned about he had met this young bright skin complexioned guy some four or five years earlier that was traveling and slumming in Fayetteville, North Carolina. Turk immediately knew who he was referring to and told Green-Eyes that it was me and that I was his Bro-n-law and directed him to my store in Mississippi.

I was out in the streets kicking it about the town and was able to because things had gotten back to the point to where I was at an ease and was making waves again. I was taking small steps with the intentions of being careful and not letting my name get out like that again that I was pushing weight. I'm in Moss Point on Jackson St. smoking and drinking with the fella's when Janice paged me and said that somebody from North Carolina that said Turk had sent them over to me was at the store and wanted to see me. My mind was like what the hell is going on and who could this be. My first thought was that maybe it was one of the road playa's passing through and Turk had told them to holla at me on the way to their destination.

Fifteen minutes later I pulled up at my store in a candy-blue, '87 Maxima with the Kaminari kit, five star Fittipaldi rims sitting on low profiles Fuji tires, gold finder trims with a black rag top and gold buttons. This was my toy and it was the cleanest ride in the county. The one's that remember it can't and won't dispute it was hard to touch at that time. It was cleaner than my Benz, Jag, Cadillac and Lincoln. It didn't carry the prestige that some of the others had but it was just as clean when it came to the 'hood and in a class of its own.

When I stepped out of the car dressed in a silk short set, bally shoes with my kango hat half cocked and seen the individual standing before me, I knew exactly who he was. He was not looking nearly as fresh and energetic as he was the last I seen of him. Something had happened to change his life in a major way and I knew just what it was because it had become something I so recognized.

Green-Eyes looked at me and I could see the astonishment in his eyes of the transformation both our lives had taken since our last encounter. The way I'm standing is a reflection as to how I was given and taught the game. You're supposed to dress and ride like a playa. It's called the sign of money. Getting money and stacking it back at the house while traveling the highway. Green-eyes was looking at the result of my hustling skills. I'm becoming the man I set out to be - rich. I was always meeting people in other states and at the time of the meeting I may be riding in an old bucket of a car but very presentable. The people I sometimes meet would have no idea how I was living and riding back in my home city. It was as if I was a local celebrity.

Green-Eyes was flabbergasted at what he saw before him. We talked for about an hour and he told me all about his fall with no shame. He asked could I get him an eight ball and that's when I recalled the look in his eyes of amazement. He had been hoping from first encounter that I would be able to point him in the direction of some crack cocaine. For old time sake I hooked him up on the house, didn't cost him a dime. Further evidence of the playa I had become. I've asked people over the years that were from North Carolina and some in the Fayetteville area had they ever heard of a guy that went by the name of Green-Eyes. Yes, he was a true legend in that part of the Country and well known for his pimping.

I got deep back into the dope game and excelled to a level that very few have and will ever know. I went beyond hood-rich status. I paid a helluva price for this status and venture in my life which I may, or may not, write about in a second true story of my life. To the readers, I appreciate your support and time taken to read my voice and would like to leave you all with a thought. If you could not find the understanding, hated or been one of the victims mentioned in my story and was caught in the net of the slum game. I say this, don't hate the Coast Playa; hate the game.

ABOUT THE AUTHOR

The Author was born and raised in Moss Point/Pascagoula Mississippi to a large middle class family of Dubose's on his Mother side and the Chestang's on his Father side. The direction I chose in life as this story is being told is no reflection of the rearing and education given to be able to distinguish between right or wrong I knew better. The Universal laws, your rational and irrational decisions can dictate and determine your out-come in life.

The path and directions you travel may allow you to find yourself and come into a conscious understanding of your existence and who you are as well as your purpose in this world. Some decisions can be detrimental and not worth the price you pay in the end. The decisions I made in my life cost me dearly when I could have done better with the gift and ability I was given by GOD. I was indicted as the leader of one of the largest cocaine conspiracy enterprises to ever originate in the Southern District of Mississippi at that time as detailed in the book "It Is What It Is" By Gerald Duffy.

I have served more than 20 years in federal prison and at the time of the publishing of Coast Playa's I await the Court's decision whether to grant me immediate release based on a new retroactive crack cocaine Amendment to the Federal Sentencing Guidelines. I hope my story has the impact of discouraging you from choosing the street life as oppose to becoming a law abiding decent human being. The decisions I made lead me to a dead end road of catastrophe. The choice is yours and you do have one. I'm a living testimony that the price is too high. The definition of insanity is, to continue with the same reckless behavior while expecting a different result....Which are you?????